THE BARBARA CARTLAND ETERNAL COLLECTION

The Barbara Cartland Eternal Collection is the unique opportunity to collect all five hundred of the timeless beautiful romantic novels written by the world's most celebrated and enduring romantic author.

Named the Eternal Collection because Barbara's inspiring stories of pure love, just the same as love itself, the books will be published on the internet at the rate of four titles per month until all five hundred are available.

The Eternal Collection, classic pure romance available worldwide for all time .

I0626610

THE LATE DAME BARBARA CARTLAND

Barbara Cartland, who sadly died in May 2000 at the grand age of ninety eight, remains one of the world's most famous romantic novelists. With worldwide sales of over one billion, her outstanding 723 books have been translated into thirty six different languages, to be enjoyed by readers of romance globally.

Writing her first book 'Jigsaw' at the age of 21, Barbara became an immediate bestseller. Building upon this initial success, she wrote continuously throughout her life, producing bestsellers for an astonishing 76 years. In addition to Barbara Cartland's legion of fans in the UK and across Europe, her books have always been immensely popular in the USA. In 1976 she achieved the unprecedented feat of having books at numbers 1 & 2 in the prestigious B. Dalton Bookseller bestsellers list.

Although she is often referred to as the 'Queen of Romance', Barbara Cartland also wrote several historical biographies, six autobiographies and numerous theatrical plays as well as books on life, love, health and cookery. Becoming one of Britain's most popular media personalities and dressed in her trademark pink, Barbara spoke on radio and television about social and political issues, as well as making many public appearances.

In 1991 she became a Dame of the Order of the British Empire for her contribution to literature and her work for humanitarian and charitable causes.

Known for her glamour, style, and vitality Barbara Cartland became a legend in her own lifetime. Best remembered for her wonderful romantic novels and loved by millions of readers worldwide, her books remain treasured for their heroic heroes, plucky heroines and traditional values. But above all, it was Barbara Cartland's overriding belief in the positive power of love to help, heal and improve the quality of life for everyone that made her truly unique.

THE AUDACIOUS ADVENTURESS

Barbara Cartland

Barbara Cartland Ebooks Ltd

This edition © 2019

ISBNs

9781788672078   EPUB

9781788672085   PAPERBACK

Book design by M-Y Books
m-ybooks.co.uk

CHAPTER ONE
1802

The door opened and a gentleman slipped hastily into the room and locked the door behind him.

As he turned, he saw that a woman rising from a table by the window was watching him with a white frightened face.

"Don't be alarmed," he said to her reassuringly, "I am but taking refuge in here for a moment."

As he spoke, he saw to his surprise that the expression on her face, which had almost been one of terror, changed to one of relief.

Then, as he walked towards her, he felt that there was something like recognition in the smile on her lips and the look in her eyes before she settled herself once again at the table and picked up her embroidery.

A memory stirred in the back of the gentleman's mind.

"I seem to know you! Could we have met before?"

It seemed impossible. The gentleman, tall, broad-shouldered and exceedingly handsome, was attired in the height of fashion, his blue satin evening coat fitted without a wrinkle, the points of his collar reached high against his square jaw and the elegance of his snowy cravat must have taken an infinity of patience to achieve.

The woman he faced, or rather she was little more than a girl, was unassuming to the point of mediocrity. Her hair was dragged back from her forehead into a tightly plaited bun at the nape of her neck.

Her gown, drab and out-dated, was of some cheap dark material and, when she had sprung to her feet at the unexpected appearance of a stranger, she had reached out for a pair of spectacles that lay beside her on the table.

Now it appeared that she had no use for them. She replaced them before she picked up her needle and started to embroider skilfully and quickly on a gown of pale pink crêpe.

"Why should I know you?" the gentleman asked musingly as she made no reply.

She looked up at him again with a little mischievous twinkle in her eyes that were unexpectedly large in the light of the candles she was working by and seemed to be almost green.

"Of course!" the gentleman exclaimed. "You are Druscilla! Good God! You are the last person I expected to find here.'

"I am honoured that you recognise me, Cousin Valdo," she replied demurely.

The Marquis of Lynche pulled up a chair to the table and sat himself down on it.

"Druscilla, by all that is Holy!" he said. "I have often wondered what became of you."

"Papa left Lynche Hall after your mother died," Druscilla replied. "He quarrelled with the next Marchioness."

"Who did not?" the Marquis exclaimed. "But where did you go?"

"To Ovington, as it happened, on His Grace's estate," Druscilla responded. "Until Papa also passed away."

"My condolences," the Marquis said conventionally. "But why are you here?"

"I am Governess to Her Grace's small daughter."

"A Governess!" the Marquis declared. "Is there nothing better you can do?"

She gave a little smile that had a touch of cynicism in it.

"And what do you suggest," she asked, "for a female orphan without money and without influence?"

"The family would have helped you," he interrupted.

"Papa had cut himself off from all Mama's relations," she replied. "He always felt that they looked down on him and resented his having married into the Nobility. And so I have had no communication with my grand connections."

"That is nonsensical!" the Marquis expostulated. "Your father might choose to set himself aloof, but you are different, you are my cousin."

"The relationship is not close," Druscilla retorted coldly. "My grandmother was your grandmother's sister. We are second cousins if you like, but it is not a relationship of blood."

"But nevertheless, we are related," the Marquis told her sternly. "Something must be done about your position."

"Your interference is not necessary," Druscilla answered. "And please don't tell anyone that I am here. For the moment everything is satisfactory."

"What do you mean 'for the moment'?" the Marquis enquired.

Druscilla hesitated and then she said in a low voice,

"Things have not been very easy and it will not help if anyone should find you in the schoolroom. For goodness sake, Valdo, now you have seen me, go away and forget it."

"Why should I?" he asked her. "Besides, I have a reason for coming here."

"What is it?" Druscilla demanded sharply and he saw an echo of the fear that had been so apparent in her face when he had first entered the room.

Then, as if in answer to her question, a sudden pandemonium broke out in the corridor. There were the strains of a hunting horn, masculine laughter and shouts of 'Tally Ho!' and 'Gone Away!', high-spirited female screams and the thunder of feet running past the door.

The Marquis noted that Druscilla sat tense and still, only one small hand crept up to her breast as if to quell a turmoil within herself.

Then the noise became deafening.

Suddenly the handle of the door was turned violently and the door rattled as someone tried to force it open.

A female voice shrieked,

"It's locked, he cannot be there!"

Again the hunting horn blared out and the cries of 'Gone Away!' gradually faded as the crowd of merrymakers progressed down the corridor.

"You see why I have gone to ground," the Marquis smiled.

"Are they chasing you?" Druscilla asked.

"Two of us were chosen," he replied, "both eligible bachelors. My God, Druscilla, I assure you that after this a fox has all my sympathy."

"Why did you agree to do it?" she enquired.

"How could I refuse? Not without making a cake of myself, and I have learnt that in such circumstances, Druscilla, it is far better to agree what people want of one and then to do the opposite."

She gave a little laugh.

"You always did get your own way, Valdo, with never a thought that other people might suffer in consequence."

"What do you mean by that?" he asked.

"Only that last holiday at Lynche Hall when I was punished after you had gone back to Eton because it was my ball you had thrown through the greenhouse!"

"Poor Druscilla," he commiserated, "and I bet you never sneaked on me."

"No, I did not, as it happens, which was foolish of me. The heir of the house would have been forgiven for his crime, whatever it might be, while I was only the tomboy daughter of the local Vicar."

"What happened to you?" the Marquis wanted to know.

"Oh, a good spanking and bread and water for supper, it was nothing new," she answered lightly.

"You must accept my apologies for my past sins."

"The only apology I would appreciate," she replied, "is that you should leave this room. Go and go quickly."

"Why are you so anxious to be rid of me?"

"Because someone might find you here. Can you imagine what will be said? Besides, Her Grace only engaged me on condition that – "

She stopped suddenly.

"Will you not finish that sentence?" the Marquis prompted her.

It seemed as though his question aroused her anger.

"Very well, I will finish it," she said, her eyes flashing. "Her Grace engaged me on condition that, I did not indulge in any philandering while I was under her roof."

"Philandering!"

"If you think that I want to philander with a gentleman of your type, you are mistaken," she insisted. "They have one use and one use only for a woman. Men are beasts – every one of them. The less I see of them the better for my peace of mind!"

Druscilla's lips closed in a hard line and, with something suspiciously like a sob, she picked up her discarded embroidery.

"Go away, Valdo," she said more quietly, "And forget you have seen me."

"Some man has hurt you," he commented. "Who could have treated you in such a manner? Who?"

She gave a laugh with no humour in it.

"Not one man, my dear cousin, but the father, the son, the uncle and the distinguished friend they did not want to offend – the lot! Each one as bad as the other, all out for a bit of fun round the corner, knowing the wretched girl they insulted would not dare to complain and if anything was discovered, their word would be believed against hers."

"It sounds incredible," the Marquis remarked.

"You don't believe me?" Druscilla went on. "Do you imagine it is pleasant to be hounded away from six different situations in three years? Six! And then to have to come crawling on my knees to be taken in here and to be engaged as a great condescension – an act of charity."

She stopped speaking and looked at him.

"*Now* do you understand? Now will you go away and not ruin my last chance of living a decent life unmolested?"

The Marquis rose to his feet. His face was troubled.

"I will go, Druscilla, because you have asked it of me, but I shall not forget. I will speak to the family. You should not be allowed to suffer like this."

"Leave me alone," she snapped. "I don't want the charity of my relations any more than I want anyone else's. They looked down their noses at Mama because she had married a Parson and they will not take any more kindly to me. Put me out of your mind, Valdo. You have not remembered my existence these last nine years and there is no reason why it should trouble you now."

"Nine years! Good Lord! Is it as long as that?" the Marquis exclaimed. "But it is not right, Druscilla, that you – "

The words died because there came a knock on the door.

Druscilla jumped to her feet and he saw again that look of terror on her face. He put a finger to his lips and then tiptoed across the room, opening a door at the far end.

He guessed it led into a bedroom and his assumption was right.

By the light of the flickering night light he could see a child sleeping in a small narrow bed. By the side of it was another bed that obviously belonged to Druscilla.

The Marquis pushed the door to behind him, leaving only a faint chink through which he could see and hear what went on in the schoolroom.

Druscilla moved slowly across the room to the door and, as she reached it, the knock came again.

"Who is it?" she asked and he heard a faint tremor in her voice.

"'Tis me, Miss Morley," a woman's voice replied.

"Oh, Miss Deane!"

He heard the relief in Druscilla's tone as she turned the key in the lock and opened the door. Through the crack that he had left himself the Marquis could see a fat middle-aged woman in a mob-cap, obviously an elderly housemaid, carry a tray across the room and set it down on the table.

"I've brought your supper, Miss Morley."

"How kind of you," Druscilla exclaimed.

"I took the tray from Ellen," the housemaid explained. "The girl was half-dead on her feet so I sent her off to bed. I'm goin' to have a sharp word with the kitchen tomorrow. They've no right to keep her hangin' about there so long or to be so late with your meal."

"I expect they are busy," Druscilla said, "and I am not really hungry."

"If you're not, you ought to be," Miss Deane said sharply. "You've been a-workin' away at that gown all day. And it looks as though you've still got quite a lot to do."

"I should be finished in another three hours," Druscilla said with a little sigh. "Her Grace wants to wear it tomorrow."

"To please her new beau, I'll be bound," Miss Deane said with a laugh. "Well, I can understand her wantin' to do that. I've never set eyes on a finer lookin' and more handsome-countenanced gentleman than the Marquis. It makes my old heart beat just to look at him. And his Lordship's a vast improvement, I may say, on Her Grace's last fancy."

"Indeed."

Druscilla's voice was cold and the Marquis realised that she was embarrassed.

The housemaid did not appear to notice and went on,

"Yes, to be sure! Sir Andrew Blackett, now he was a real horror. I couldn't let any of my young maids go near his bedchamber. I knew his type as soon as I sees him! And when young Gladys came to me a-cryin' her eyes out, I felt like givin' him a piece of my mind, I did really."

"I don't blame you," Druscilla murmured.

"And, of course, it was due to him that poor Miss Lovelace got turned away without a reference."

"Is that why she went?"

"It was indeed. Her Grace finds him in here, a-talkin' to Miss Lovelace. Just before dinner it was. Of course he says that he came to say 'goodnight' to her little Ladyship, but Her Grace sees that Miss Lovelace is lookin' flushed and pleased with the attention she's a-havin'. So as soon as the party is over out she goes."

"It was not fair, was it?" Druscilla asked, a note of anger in her voice,

"Mistresses don't trouble themselves as to what is fair when you're in service," Miss Deane replied. "And if anything's wrong, 'tis never the gentry that's at fault. You can make up your mind about that! I can see that you are wise, Miss Morley, in that you locks your door. Well, you keep it locked day and night while there's this sort of party's goin' on in the house."

"You think I should protect myself from the Marquis?" Druscilla asked, a note of mischief in her voice that the listener in the bedroom could detect quite clearly.

"Well, you never knows, do you," Miss Deane answered. "But 'tis not the Marquis that I'd be wary of tonight, not with His Grace away! There's others in the party who'll not be so preoccupied. Nevertheless the Marquis has a reputation for being a high-stepper when it comes to the female sex."

"Has he indeed," Druscilla murmured curiously.

"One of the valets has been makin' us laugh fit to split our sides downstairs durin' supper," Miss Deane explained. "He was tellin' us how his Lordship, to escape from a jealous husband, once shinned down a drainpipe only to fall into a water butt."

"That must have cooled his ardour," Druscilla smiled.

"And another time," Miss Deane went on with relish, "he only avoided discovery by a-creepin' out of the back door with a chef's hat on his head. Oh, he's a real dasher and no mistake! Of course his Lordship's own man sat there with pursed lips sayin' nothin', but I knew by the twinkle in his eyes that the stories were not all that exaggerated."

"You really think I am safe from this rapacious Lothario?" Druscilla asked.

"Well, I don't know what you means by that," Miss Deane said, "but they says he's absolutely infatuated with Her Grace and she with him. From what the pantry was a-sayin', she was holdin' his hand under the table at dinner and castin' him such languishin' glances that it was quite difficult to serve the dishes, their heads were so close together."

"Well, it's certainly a good thing that His Grace is away," Drucilla said.

"It is indeed," Miss Deane agreed. "We all knows what His Grace's temper is like when it's aroused. One of the coachmen was sayin' only the other day that His Grace can be a nasty customer when he's in one of his rages like someone he wouldn't want to encounter on a dark night."

Druscilla gave a little gurgle of laughter.

"Oh, Miss Deane, you are funny."

"But there I mustn't stand talkin' to you," Miss Deane said. "There's a dozen jobs awaitin' and me short-handed with Ellen going off to bed. Goodnight, Miss Morley, and keep the door looked."

"I will indeed," Druscilla answered, "and thank you again for bringing my supper."

She turned the key in the lock after the housemaid had left the room.

As the Marquis emerged from the bedroom, she greeted him with a mischievous smile.

"Druscilla, you little Devil!" he accused her in a low voice. "You led her on deliberately to discomfort me! Do they always talk like that below stairs?"

"Of course they do," Druscilla answered. "There is nothing that escapes their eyes not even when people hold hands under the table."

"*Damn it!*" the Marquis exclaimed. "It makes me feel such a fool."

"Remember that they are only servants and beneath your condescension," Druscilla advised him. "And now for Heaven's sake go away in case someone finds you here. You heard what happened to Miss Lovelace."

"I gather she was the last Governess."

"I look her place," Druscilla said, her voice suddenly serious. "Poor thing, I wonder what will happen to her Without references it's almost impossible to find any employment."

The Marquis reached the door and turned the key cautiously.

"Goodnight, Druscilla, you have given me a great deal to think about. And this is not the last you will see of me."

"Then I shall be disappointed," she replied sharply. "You can do nothing for me, my dear cousin, except leave me alone."

He smiled at her and she was forced to admit to herself that he was a beguiling young man and it was no wonder that so many foolish women risked their reputations for him.

She listened to his feet going down the passage and then relocking the door she settled herself once again at the table with her embroidery.

She glanced at the tray that Miss Meadows had brought her and saw that it contained a rather unappetising leg of chicken, a piece of cheese and a hastily cut crust of bread.

The food was not usually so scanty or so badly served, but, when there was a large party in the house, the staff were strained to their uttermost to cope with the extra amount of work there was to do.

It was not only the number of guests, she had heard Miss Deane earlier in the day say that about twenty-five people would be staying.

But, as each of the visitors brought their lady's maid, their valet, their coachman, their footmen and sometimes even other members of their staff, it meant that the housemaids were working from dusk until late into the night without extra help.

But it was not of the difficulties of the house nor of her unappetising meal that Druscilla was thinking about as she put down her embroidery once again and stared across the room.

She was thinking of the Marquis and how different he looked today from the overgrown youth he had been when she last saw him.

It was now 1802 so he must have been seventeen that last summer at Lynche Hall, she thought, while she had just passed her tenth birthday.

He had been bored because his mother was ill and there were no parties in the Big House. And so he had been quite amused to have as a companion a small girl who had followed him about adoringly, ready to fetch and carry or, as he had called it, *fag* for him.

He teased her incessantly, she remembered, because she had red hair.

"Come on, Carrots! Where are you, Ginger?" was the usual way he had addressed her.

And she had loved it, happy to follow him through the woods when he went out pigeon shooting and proud to be allowed to carry home his game for him.

He had taken her boating on the lake and upset the boat by mistake so that she had gone home looking like a drowned rat.

They had stolen the best peaches from the greenhouses when the Head Gardener was not looking and sat in the sun to eat them with a delicious feeling of guilt.

He dared her to walk along the top of the high brick walls and while she quaked with the fear of falling and breaking her neck, she had never let him see that she was afraid.

On horseback she followed him over jumps that she would never have dared to attempt if she had not feared that he would laugh at her for being a coward. And when her father had given up the incumbency at Lynche, she remembered thinking despairingly that she would never see Cousin Valdo again.

And now, she thought, he had grown just like all the other men she had met since she had left home, overdressed, foppish, conceited and interested in nothing but chasing after women and making life unbearable for their inferiors.

"I hate him!" she said aloud.

She was all the more incensed because he had disturbed her, taking away the feeling of peace and security that she had found in the schoolroom and bringing back all too vividly the terrors she had endured these last two and a half years since her father's death.

She supposed that it was because she had been brought up in the quiet and peace of a Vicarage that she had found the world that she had been pitchforked into so horrifying.

Her innocence had made her find the attentions of those who thrust themselves upon her not only distasteful but evil.

She had been panic-stricken not once but half a dozen times to the point when she felt that life was too frightening for her to wish to go on living.

Then gradually her contempt for those who insulted her had given her a new strength and a fresh resilience to fight them with.

Nevertheless it had been a very different kind of fear that had brought her to The Castle to plead with the Duchess for a position in her household.

Without references there was not a Domestic Bureau left that would take her on their books and she had to face the fact that she might soon have to surrender herself to one of the gentlemen who continually importuned her.

'I would rather die,' she told herself not once but a hundred times until it became the truth.

Then she thought that she would take a wild gamble and throw herself on the Duchess's mercy. It meant spending all that remained of her money on a seat in the stagecoach that passed The Castle gates.

It was by sheer chance that she turned up just as Miss Lovelace had been dismissed and the. Duchess had no one else in mind. And she had been frank about the difficulties that she had encountered in her previous positions.

The Duchess had been equally frank.

"I will employ you on the strict understanding, Miss Morley, that there will be no philandering in this house. Neither His Grace nor I would tolerate that sort of behaviour."

"There will be nothing like that, Your Grace," Druscilla had asserted firmly.

Even as she spoke, she thought despairingly of what had happened in her other posts and of the men who had crept along to the schoolroom at night.

Men who had removed the key so that she could not lock the door, of the expression in their eyes the moment they had seen her, their hands going out to touch her, to pull her to them, their lips seeking hers and their laughter when she struggled against them.

'Men, men, I loathe them all,' she told herself, 'and Valdo is only another of them!'

With a little sigh she realised that the Duchess' gown would not be ready by morning if she did not go to work.

It was not the job of a Governess to embroider for her Mistress or indeed to do any of the work that should have been done by a lady's maid, but, once Her Grace had discovered how skilfully Druscilla sewed, there were always extra tasks waiting on the schoolroom table for her.

And perhaps, Druscilla had thought despairingly more than once, this would be a compelling reason for the Duchess to wish to keep her.

Nevertheless her back ached and her heart was still pounding a little because Valdo had come to the schoolroom and raised the fear of his being discovered there.

Had one of the servants had a sight of him leaving or entering the room, Druscilla was well aware that the Duchess would know the next morning.

They were all frightened of Her Grace's spy, the Groom of the Chambers. He read the blotting paper in the guest rooms by holding it up to the mirror, he searched the wastepaper baskets and he listened at keyholes. There was little he did not know and nothing happened, however trivial, that he did not transmit to Her Grace.

Druscilla felt herself shiver at the thought and, feeling suddenly cold, she went to the bedroom and, taking off her dress, slipped on her nightgown and her warm flannel dressing gown.

Then she let down her hair, releasing it from its tight bun. It cascaded over her shoulders like a flood of fiery gold, rippling down until it reached far below her waist.

Moving across the bedroom and shading with one hand the candle she carried so as not to disturb the sleeping child, Druscilla found her hairbrush and carried it into the schoolroom.

She usually brushed her hair for a hundred strokes every night, just as her mother had taught her to do, but tonight she was too tired and there was too much to be done.

She brushed it only until it sparkled as if alive and then skilfully plaited it so that it hung down her back like a schoolgirl's and tied it with a small bow of green ribbon.

Now she was ready to continue her work and yet she still felt disturbed. She looked at her meal and decided that it was not worthwhile even to try the cold chicken.

Instead she cut herself a piece of cheese, buttered a small portion of the crust of bread and tried to eat. But finding this impossible she resolutely put the tray on the other side of the room and settled down at the table.

With about six inches of the embroidery still to do, she wondered how quickly she could finish it.

She must have been working for nearly two hours when suddenly there was a sound of footsteps running down the passage.

It had been so quiet in the schoolroom that the noise was quite startling and Druscilla raised her head.

The footsteps stopped outside the door and there came a knock, followed by another.

Druscilla sat still as if turned to stone.

Then she heard a voice hardly above a whisper.

"Druscilla, it's me, Valdo. For God's sake open the door."

Her instinct told her to refuse and yet somehow, almost as though she was compelled against her will, Druscilla rose from the table and crossed the room.

"What is it?" she asked.

"Let me in, I beg of you. Please, Druscilla!"

Again she would have refused, but there was something in his voice and the urgency of it that compelled her.

She turned the key and he burst open the door almost knocking her down.

"Quick," he urged her, "go back to the table. If anyone comes, I have been here for the past hour talking to you about the old days. Do you understand?"

"What has – happened?" she asked.

"Only you can help me," he replied. "I beg of you, Druscilla. I am desperate or I would not ask it of you."

She hesitated and then they both heard a sound in the distance.

"Quick, do as I ask," he said. "You cannot fail me, Druscilla, you never have!"

It was these last words that decided her. With a swiftness that surprised even herself, she rushed back to the table and picked up her discarded embroidery.

As she did so, the Marquis pushed a chair in front of the table and threw himself down on it, his feet raised on another.

It was then she realised for the first time that he carried his coat over his arm and that he wore no cravat. His white lawn shirt was open at the neck and his hair, meticulously arranged earlier in the evening in the windswept style affected by the Prince Regent, was now ruffled and dishevelled.

There was no time to tell him so for he threw both his coat and his waistcoat down on the floor and started to fasten his cuffs. Even as he did so the door was thrown open and the Duke of Windleham stood there.

His Grace was in his travelling clothes, his polished riding boots slightly bespeckled with mud and, as Druscilla rose automatically to her feet, she saw with a sudden constriction of her heart that His Grace was in one of his rages.

There was no mistaking the fury in his dark eyes or the way his eyebrows met in a heavy frown across his nose.

The Marquis did not move from his comfortable position, but Druscilla knew that he was tense as he looked across the room at His Grace.

"Are you prepared to fight me, Lynche?" the Duke asked. "Or do I get my lackeys to throw you from the house?"

The Marquis rose very slowly to his feet.

"I am, of course, delighted to oblige you, Windleham," he said slowly, "but for what reason I have yet to discover."

"The reason is obvious, is it not?" the Duke asked and his voice was like a lash. "I saw you leaving my wife's bedroom as I approached it."

"My dear Windleham, what a nonsensical suggestion," the Marquis replied. "I assure you that I have been here for the past hour talking to my cousin, Druscilla, and she will confirm that it is the truth."

"I prefer, Lynche, to believe what I have seen with my own eyes," the Duke replied. "You will fight me or I will call my footmen."

He had hardly finished speaking when there was a scream and the Duchess swept into the room. She was wearing a diaphanous negligée of pale sapphire-blue chiffon and her golden hair fell to her shoulders. She looked exceedingly lovely even in her distress.

"George, what are you saying?" she demanded. "Are you crazed? I assure you that the Marquis has not been in my room although what he is doing here I cannot conceive."

She looked around in quite genuine surprise.

"My dear," the Duke answered, "this homely little scene is, I am convinced, contrived entirely for my benefit. I saw Lynche quite clearly and what I saw only bears out the information conveyed to me on other occasions as to his behaviour where you are concerned. I have, as a gentleman of honour, challenged him to a duel and, as a gentleman of honour, he has accepted."

The Duchess stamped her foot.

"I will not have it!" she cried. "I will not have it, George! Would you ruin me? The Queen has set her face against duelling as you well know. If you kill his Lordship, you will have to go into exile and I should detest above all things to have to live in France or Italy. Besides how could I gave up my position at Court."

"That surely is something that should have crossed your mind a little earlier," the Duke sneered.

"And if the Marquis kills you," the Duchess continued without having seemed to hear his interruption, "can you imagine what my life would be? As the Dowager, I should be forced to live in the Dower House while that odious spendthrift nephew of yours inherits."

"It would be regrettable indeed," the Duke agreed, "but I don't think that Lynche will kill me, my dear."

"And if you kill him, as I have just said," the Duchess responded, "it will make things no better. I will not be fought over! Besides, as you have already been told, it was not true. You imagined what you saw. Is that not so, my Lord?"

The Duchess cast the Marquis a look of desperate appeal, looking so intensely pretty as she did so that it would have required a heart of stone to refuse her anything at that moment.

"I have already informed His Grace," the Marquis said slowly, "that I have in fact been here for the last hour talking with my cousin Druscilla. It was a great surprise to discover earlier in the evening that she was a guest in your house."

"A guest?" the Duke queried. "Miss Morley is, I believe, Governess to my daughter. And as a Governess, Miss Morley, do you usually receive gentlemen, even though they profess to be your cousins, in the early hours of the morning entertaining them while they are in a state of shall we say disarray and you are in your night attire?"

The Duke's voice seemed to vibrate across the room.

The blood coursed into Druscilla's face and then ebbed away again, leaving her very pale.

"No, Your Grace," she replied in a low voice. "It is not my habit to receive gentlemen in such a manner, but my cousin, Valdo, is rather different. We were brought up together when we were children and we were in fact just talking over old times."

The Duke looked at the clock.

"At nearly two o'clock in the morning, Miss Morley?"

There was so much insinuation in his tone that Druscilla drew in her breath sharply.

"It is true," the Duchess cried. "You may be quite certain, George, that his Lordship had something very important to impart to his cousin. Now are you satisfied?"

"I may be a greenhorn," the Duke said, "in many matters, but not in this, my dear. My offer still stands, Lynche."

"No, you cannot, you cannot mean it," the Duchess declared, turning to him and holding on to the lapels of his coat to make him look down at her. "It is true, I tell you, it is true. My Lord Marquis has told me what a partiality he had for his cousin. We have talked about it and he said how much he was looking forward to seeing her. I knew all about it, I tell you, it is true. How can you be so disbelieving?"

She turned from her husband towards the Marquis.

"Oh, my Lord," she pleaded, "make him believe you. You know how disastrous a duel would be and what it would mean to me. I pray of you to persuade His Grace that you were not with me tonight, as apparently he still believes."

There were tears in the Duchess's blue eyes and her mouth was trembling.

The Marquis took one look at her and faced the Duke.

"I am sorry if Your Grace does not credit what I have told you and perhaps you would be a little more understanding if I informed you that I was in point of fact asking my cousin Druscilla to do me the great honour of becoming my wife."

For a moment there was utter silence in the room as though everyone had been arrested to the point of stupefaction by the Marquis's words.

Then with a little twist of his lips the Duke said,

"So the much vaunted bachelor Marquis has been caught at last. May I ask what the lady in question, Miss Morley, has to say to this offer."

Three pairs of eyes turned to look at Druscilla and for a moment she saw them clearly as though they were inanimate

~19~

pictures in front of her, the Duchess's eyes pleading with her to substantiate the lie, the Marquis's almost compelling her and the Duke's suspicious, unconvinced and accusing.

They were waiting for her, all waiting for her to speak.

At last through dry lips she replied,

"Such a sincere protestation has my attention – and on thinking it over – I have naturally much pleasure in accepting the invitation of my cousin to be – his wife."

The Duchess gave a little cry.

"Then that settles it," she said. "Now, George, are you satisfied."

"Naturally, my dear," the Duke replied and then, as his audience almost visibly relaxed, he went on, "But as a father and as a Guardian of the morals and manners in this house, I cannot condone Miss Morley's behaviour in being so scantily attired even when receiving anything so momentous as an offer of marriage. It therefore behoves me to see that this Wedding takes place with all possible speed. My Chaplain shall be aroused and you, my Lord, and Miss Morley, shall be joined in Holy Matrimony within the hour."

"Married!" the Marquis expostulated.

"What do you mean, George?" the Duchess demanded almost shrilly

"I mean, my dear," the Duke answered, "that your friend, the Noble Marquis, must substantiate his story if I am to accept it and what could be more convincing than that they should be wed immediately with you and me to witness such a delightful little Ceremony?"

"It's impossible!" the Marquis exclaimed hotly.

"Then my original offer stands," the Duke retorted. "I will leave it to you to exercise the choice of weapons."

"No, no," the Duchess cried out again, "the whole thing is ridiculous and nonsensical. Think what everyone will say!"

"There is no reason why anyone should know," the Duke replied, "unless you chatter, my dear. And that I cannot believe you would do."

"Such a marriage would not be legal," the Marquis came in quickly, "one has to have a Special Licence."

"Now this may come as a surprise," the Duke said, drawing a paper from the inner pocket of his travelling coat. "The reason I posted to Oxford and was unfortunately not present to receive my guests, was that I had learnt that my nephew was on the point of making a disastrous marriage with the daughter of a tradesman. He had even gone so far as to procure a Special Licence. I took it from him to make sure that he did not use it as soon as my back was turned. And I have it here in my hand."

The Duke glanced down at it.

"The names, of course, will have to be changed, but, as His Grace the Archbishop of Canterbury is a distant relative of mine, I have no doubt that when I explain the circumstances he will not object to my action in this matter."

"Damn you, you hold every ace, do you not?" the Marquis raged.

The Duke's eyes then met his across the room.

"It is wise of you to acknowledge it," the Duke replied.

He turned towards Druscilla.

"Miss Morley, you will oblige me by getting decently robed and I imagine that, if I allow you an hour to do this and complete your packing, it will be enough time."

"My packing?" Druscilla queried in a bewildered tone.

"But of course," the Duke replied suavely, "you will wish to leave The Castle with your husband. He also should have no difficulty in being ready at the same time. The Chapel, as I expect you know, is in the West wing. We will wait for you there. And now, my dear," he said taking the Duchess's arm, "you and I will repair to our rooms."

"It's mad, George, absolutely mad!" the Duchess almost shouted at him.

"I am sorry you should think so," the Duke replied. "I think actually it is a very sane and civilised way of solving what might have proved to be, from your point of view, a bitter tragedy."

His words checked anything further that the Duchess might have said. Instead she allowed herself to be led meekly from the schoolroom with just one backward glance of pleading at the Marquis.

He watched her out of sight and then glanced at Druscilla, who was staring at him white-faced and trembling.

"*God!* What a monstrous tangle!" he flashed. "Why the Devil didn't you refuse me, you stupid chit?"

CHAPTER TWO

"*Damn him, may his soul rot in hell! Curse him! Blast him!*"

The Marquis flung himself back against the soft cushions of the coach, the oaths pouring from his lips and growing more profane, more violent and more obscene.

It was only after a few minutes of losing control of himself that he realised the small figure beside him was sitting completely still and upright.

It flashed through his mind that another woman would have screamed out at his profanity or closed her ears against his violence.

The words died away on his lips and in the light of the lantern he had another look at the silent figure beside him.

'Good Lord,' he thought to himself, 'She looks like some upper servant.'

The thought made him swear again.

"God Almighty!" he shouted out aloud. "I shall be the laughing stock of St. James's! Can you not see how they will snigger and crow over me? 'The Bachelor Marquis', the man who had originated his own Bachelor Club with a forfeit of five hundred guineas for any member who marries. And the only excuse for entering the bonds of Matrimony would be if one had been completely bowled over by – "

He stopped suddenly realising that he was being unnecessarily insulting.

After all Druscilla was his cousin and the only redeeming feature in this whole nightmare was that she was of gentle blood and not, as might well have happened, just some common nonentity.

At the same time she was not the sort of wife a man could produce proudly or who could, as he had been about to say, suggest by her appearance a convincing excuse for the surrender of bachelorhood.

However, because he could not help being somewhat ashamed of his behaviour, he said somewhat ungraciously,

"I suppose that I should apologise to you."

"There is no need – to do so," Druscilla replied in a clear calm voice that was somehow more irritating than if she had been distraught or upset.

Then, moving it seemed for the first time since she had entered the coach, she took her spectacles from her eyes and, lifting the sash of the window frame, opened it a few inches to throw the spectacles out onto the road.

"Why have you done that?" the Marquis asked curiously.

"A symbolic gesture," she replied and he saw her smile in the flickering light of the candle."

"Symbolic of what?" he asked.

"The fact that I shall need them no longer," Druscilla answered. "I wore them merely to make myself more unprepossessing – and less likely to attract attention."

"Was that really necessary?" the Marquis enquired.

He wondered as he asked the question why he must continue to be so disagreeable to this girl, who after all had obliged him in a desperate situation.

But, as he had taken his vows in the Chapel of The Castle, vows that he had to force almost through gritted teeth, he could not help contrasting the bride who stood at his side with the voluptuous beauty of the woman he loved.

It was impossible not to contrast them. The Duchess, forced undoubtedly against her will to be a witness to this unhappy marriage, had looked her most beautiful.

Only a woman would have realised that she was vastly overdressed and that the diamonds flashing against her white skin and the low décollete of her expensive evening gown were not in the best taste.

But her fair hair shone in the light of the candles on the altar and it seemed to the Marquis that her blue eyes were misty with unshed tears and her red lips more provocative than ever.

It had been hard to drag his eyes away from her to look at the drab figure that stood beside him.

Druscilla's shapeless gown was of a hideous shade of dark brown and her hair was almost obscured by an untrimmed bonnet of cheap straw. She wore glasses and he thought for a moment when she entered the Chapel that she looked like some charity wench from an orphanage.

Was it any wonder, he asked himself now, that he could think only of the ridicule he must encounter from his contemporaries? And yet some decency in him compelled him to say again,

"I am sorry, Druscilla, I should not have dragged you into this."

"There was nothing else – you could do, was there?" she replied. "Besides there is no need to be sorry for me. You have given me something – I have waited for for a long time."

"What is that?" he asked.

"The chance to become – an adventuress," she replied surprisingly.

"A what?"

"An adventuress," she repeated. "I asked Papa once what was the correct definition of an adventuress and he said it was 'a woman who was looking for – an opportunity'. Well, I have been looking for an opportunity to escape from the type of life I have been leading for some time. I am grateful to you, Valdo, for offering me the chance – to escape."

"Well, I am gratified that someone is pleased," the Marquis said surlily. "I suppose that was your only reason for accepting me."

"The alternative," Druscilla replied almost bitterly, "was to be turned out of the house without a reference. In which case, without any chance of further employment, it meant starvation or a life of sin."

The Marquis was shamed into silence and the carriage rumbled on for at least a mile before she said quietly,

"If you have got over your rage, I have a suggestion to make. Are you prepared to – listen?"

"There is nothing much else I can do, is there?" he asked irritably. "We have about an hour's drive in this cursed coach before we reach the Posting inn."

"It was kind of His Grace to suggest it all the same."

"He did not do it on our account, I can assure you," the Marquis replied. "He said to me, 'I have no desire for my guests to see you leaving The Castle with a female, which might happen if you drove your phaeton. I shall therefore have you conveyed in one of my own coaches until you are no longer on my property. There your own vehicle and grooms can meet you and after that you can go to the Devil as far as I am concerned'!"

The Marquis's voice sharpened at the last words and then he muttered,

"I wish to God I could have fought him."

"He would have killed you!"

"What do you mean?" the Marquis asked angrily. "I am considered a crack shot."

"I am convinced that you are not as – dead-eyed as the Duke," Druscilla answered, "and besides he has had a certain amount of practice. They say he killed a man in a duel five years ago. But the victim was not a person of any importance – so there was no scandal."

"What were they fighting about?" the Marquis enquired.

Druscilla laughed.

"Need you really ask that question? You are not the first man who has been infatuated by Her Grace's blue eyes nor, I am convinced, will you be the last."

"You dislike her, do you not?" the Marquis suggested.

"She is hard, jealous, mean – and petty."

She spoke coolly without any rancour in her voice.

"I don't believe you," the Marquis countered.

"I did not expect you would," Druscilla replied. "But nevertheless, she is slightly better than many of the other Ladies of Quality I have encountered. And they in their turn have more to recommend them than their husbands."

"I can see that you will fare well in the Society life you are now entering," the Marquis commented rudely.

"It was that which I wish to discuss with you."

"Have you any suggestions?" the Marquis enquired. "They will have to be good ones if we are not to be funnier than the clowns at Barnum's Fair."

"There is one thing we need not be," Druscilla retorted, "and that is – a laughing stock."

"You try and prevent it," the Marquis said despondently.

"I have every intention of doing just that," Druscilla explained. "Wait until you hear my idea."

"I am certainly prepared to listen," he replied, moving into the corner of the carriage and stretching out his legs.

He was, although Druscilla did not realise it, making a stupendous effort to control the rage and frustration that made him long to hit or smash something.

Druscilla glanced towards him.

There was no doubt that even in a tantrum he was exceedingly handsome, his broad shoulders, his clean-cut almost classical features and the way that his hair grew square on his forehead made him, as she well knew, irresistible to any woman.

Besides that there was an air of raffishness about him, a kind of dare-devilment that women have found attractive since the beginning of time.

"Well," he said as she did not speak, "are you suggesting that we set off in a sailing ship for China or that we face with proud indifference the ruinous whispering and the sniggers that await us in London?"

"I have been thinking about it very carefully," Druscilla replied, "and I think if we are clever we can avoid all the things that you are so afraid of."

"Afraid?" the Marquis echoed sharply as if the words touched him on the raw.

"Yes, of course, you are afraid," Druscilla continued, "afraid of being made to look a fool, afraid of people getting to know that you have been forced up the aisle, not at the point of a pistol, but because a woman pleaded with you to save her reputation."

The Marquis did not speak and Druscilla said suddenly,

"How could you be so cork-brained?"

"It seemed so safe," the Marquis replied, almost as though he was talking to one of his men friends rather than to a woman. "When Celeste told me that the Duke was away for the night, it seemed a Heaven-sent opportunity. It is not easy for us to see each other in London, he always seems to be around. When he said that he had to go to Oxford, it never crossed my mind that he might return early."

"You don't suppose that the whole Castle did not know that you were Her Grace's latest flirt, do you?"

"They knew before the party?" the Marquis asked in astonishment.

"But of course. Long before you arrived they were discussing it and I am convinced that the Duke's valet had informed him – every time you met Her Grace in London."

"But how could he have known?" the Marquis enquired.

"He is very friendly with Her Grace's lady's maid, in fact they are what you might call 'walking out' together."

"Oh, my God! Servants, servants!" the Marquis exclaimed. "But you should not have been gossiping with them, Druscilla."

"Who else was I supposed to talk to?" she came back harshly. "The chattering of a six-year-old child does not make for companionship or interesting conversation."

"So *that* is how he knew," the Marques said, obviously not having listened to Druscilla's defence of herself.

"And that is why he came back," Druscilla concluded.

"All right, I must have been deranged," the Marquis agreed sourly. "And I suppose from all you have told me that, even if the Duke and the Duchess do not talk, the servants will gossip."

Druscilla shook her head.

"I spoke to the Duke just when we were leaving," she said, "and he promised me that he would inform his valet and the Duchess's maid that if one whisper of what has occurred this night reached anyone else's ears, he would dismiss them without a reference. They will not risk that, as I well know."

"You think of everything, do you not," the Marquis muttered in a disagreeable voice. "What other suggestions have you to make, Druscilla?"

"It is this. I am well aware of what you must be feeling at this moment. It is bad enough to.be forced into a marriage one does not want without having to marry someone who looks like me."

"I did not say that," the Marquis said quickly.

"You very nearly did. It was in your mind, so don't trouble to deny it."

"Very well, I will not," the Marquis remarked sulkily. "But perhaps you can make yourself look a bit more up to scratch. Pretty gowns and all their furbelows should help."

"I shall certainly try, Valdo. But, as you well know, to appear in London and announce we are married is going to cause considerable comment. Even though you thought that your affair with the Duchess was discreetly handled, I am quite certain that it has been chattered about the length and breadth of St James's and in every elegant salon in Mayfair."

The Marquis's lips set in a hard line.

"*Blast it!*" he observed after a moment's thought. "Can one have no private life?"

"Not if you live in the public's eye."

"We have always been so careful," he murmured beneath his breath.

"Really, Valdo, you are being very bird-witted. You must know that anyone as beautiful as the Duchess and who is well known for her attraction to young men is likely to be talked about whatever she does. And when she is seen constantly to cast languishing glances in the direction of someone famed, like yourself, for being a Don Juan, the liaison is certain to be a luscious titbit on everyone's lips."

"Do you always talk like this?" he asked. "I can assure you, Druscilla, now you are my wife you will have to curb your tongue and, what is more, you ought not to know about such things. It is all very well for married women to talk in such a manner, but for a girl it is shocking to say the very least."

"You forget that I am now a married woman," Druscilla retorted.

"I am not likely to forget it," the Marquis answered with a groan. "Nevertheless, married or not, watch what you say. It will do neither of us any good if people are shocked by your conversation."

"I think," Druscilla said slowly, "that if I was talking like that and at the same time was smartly gowned, looking elegant and perhaps even attractive, you would be amused rather than incensed."

The Marquis looked at her in the dim light of the dawn that was now percolating through the carriage windows.

"It is difficult to think of you except as you are now," he commented bitterly.

"And that is what I want to talk to you about. Who in the family can you take me to?"

"In the family? Are you crazed?" the Marquis asked. "I don't want them to know about it, not that they will sniff a rat when they hear that I am married."

"I don't want them to hear it yet," Druscilla observed.

"What do you mean?" he enquired.

"I am suggesting that among our relations there must be someone we can trust, someone I can stay with until we announce our engagement."

"Announce our engagement?" the Marquis repeated. "But we are married, girl, have you not realised that?"

"*Of course* I have realised it," Druscilla said, as though dealing with a rather stupid child. "Do you not see that there is no need for us to shout it from the rooftops. If we do, there is certain to be speculation. And people are not absolutely addle-pated, they know full well that you have been running after the Duchess these past three months."

"How do you know it is three months?" the Marquis interposed.

"That is when I first heard about it. It may be longer for all I know."

"Damn you and gossiping servants!" the Marquis exclaimed. "It *is* in fact about three months."

"However long it is they are going to think it rather astonishing if you come straight to London from staying at The Castle and announce that you are married to someone else."

"Of course they are going to think it astonishing," the Marquis agreed. "But what the Devil can we do about it?"

"A great deal if you will only listen to me," Druscilla assured him.

"Like all women you talk too much, but go on."

"I suggest you take me – "

She paused.

" – but, of course, I know exactly who you should take me to."

"Well?" he enquired. "To whom?"

"To Great-Aunt Shermaline, your Grandmama," Druscilla cried. "Is she still alive?"

"Of course she is still alive," the Marquis answered. "Bright as a guinea and certainly more up to snuff than most old Dowagers. She must be getting on for eighty."

"She was always the nicest of all Mama's relations," Druscilla told him. "Of course I have not seen her for years. She was the only one who did not seem to be looking down her nose at us."

"No, Grandmama would never have done that," the Marquis agreed. "She would take you down a peg if you annoyed her, but she would not sneer or make you feel inferior. That is certainly true."

"Very well then, you will take me to her."

"What are you going to do when you get there?" the Marquis asked curiously.

"I am going to ask her to help me gown myself in a decent manner, I am going to ask her to present me to the *Beau Monde*. Then in about three weeks time, perhaps longer, our engagement will be announced and – we shall be married shortly afterwards."

"Married? But we are married already," the Marquis objected.

"Who is to know that?" Druscilla asked. "And besides I have a fancy to be wed in Church with a choir and a large congregation. It is what will be expected too from The Most Noble – the most eligible – Marquis of Lynche."

"Damn it, it is the most cock-eyed idea I have ever heard," the Marquis said scornfully.

"Why?" Druscilla asked. "Answer me that."

"Well, I don't know," the Marquis admitted. "We are married, what is the point of going all through that again?"

"We have been married because the alternative was a duel when you would have been killed. We have been forced together to save the reputation of a Lady of Fashion, whose only real love is for her position at Court and for the prestige, pomp and luxury she enjoys as the wife of a Duke."

"If you talk like that about the Duchess, I shall shake you, Druscilla," the Marquis said sharply.

"All right I will not tease you," Druscilla conceded, "but I would not put it past you to shake me anyway. You hit me once with your cricket bat and I had a bruise on my leg for weeks."

"I expect you deserved it," the Marquis parried unfeelingly.

"Well, to continue. During those three weeks it would be wise if you would go away somewhere. Stay with some friends or go to the races at Newmarket, while I will do what I can to look a little more presentable and more like the sort of wife you might have chosen had you a choice."

"I still think the whole idea is crazy," the Marquis said, "but at least it decides what we shall do when we get to London. I have no desire to take you to a hotel or to arrive at Lynche House looking as you do would set a thousand tongues wagging."

"Where does your Grandmama live now?"

"Where she has always lived in a huge draughty mausoleum in Curzon Street."

"And you are sure she will be there?" Druscilla said a trifle anxiously.

"It is May and, if you think that Grandmama would miss a Season in London, you are very much mistaken. She may be old, but there is very little she does miss."

"Very well, we will go straight to Curzon Street," Druscilla announced. "We will have breakfast in the Posting inn and then you can take me there in your phaeton. By the time we reach London it will still be early in the morning. The fashionable world will be asleep, so it is unlikely that anyone will see me."

The Marquis was silent for a moment and then he said slowly,

"I am sorry, Druscilla, for my behaviour. I am not usually so rough-mouthed."

'You were under some provocation," Druscilla smiled. "Equally, as I have already told you, Valdo, there is no need to apologise."

"Of course, the adventuress!" he said with a twist of his lips. "Well, if this is your idea of adventure, all I can say is I much prefer the quiet life."

"Nonsense! You have never had a quiet life and you would not know what to do with one if you did," Druscilla declared

"How do you know?" he enquired.

"I have heard a great deal about you from different places where I have been employed," she answered. "When they mentioned your name, I kept my ears pricked. Why not? You are the only person I knew anything about in a world where most of my employers either moved or wished to move."

"What did you hear?" the Marquis asked with the irresistible curiosity of someone hearing about themselves.

"Some time I will tell you. Most of it is not particularly to your credit. My last employer, for instance, was enraged because you had enticed away his ballet dancer – a 'little bit-of-muslin' who he apparently had spent quite a considerable amount of money on until she preferred the carriage-and-pair you offered her. And, of course, there were a number of other attractions as well."

"Really, Druscilla, you should not talk about such things!" the Marquis expostulated.

"You asked me," Druscilla answered simply.

"You mean you were employed by that swine Walden?"

"No, I was employed by his wife," Druscilla replied, "to look after their two children aged five and six. Unfortunately when Lord Walden's attention was no longer engaged with the pretty ballet dancer – he looked nearer home for amusement."

"You really mean that Walden insulted you by his attentions?" the Marquis asked incredulously.

"*Insulted* is the right word," Druscilla said bitterly. "And when I escaped him I was cast out of the house at a moment's notice – and without a reference. He told his wife that I was – importuning him."

"And she believed him?" the Marquis demanded.

"Women always prefer to believe their husbands. When I protested and told her the truth, she simply refused to pay my wages."

"I cannot believe that anyone would behave like that, but Walden is an outsider, you should not have gone to his house in the first place."

"There is an old adage that says *beggars cannot be choosers*," Druscilla replied. "The position I had before I went to Lady Walden was complicated by the eldest son thinking that I was a Heaven-sent opportunity for completing his education as a seducer and lecher."

Druscilla's voice was sharp for a moment as though the memory of what had happened still hurt.

"You have had a rotten time," the Marquis then said in a very different tone, "and when I have a chance I will get even with Lord Walden! You see if I don't."

"You have already punished him," Druscilla interposed, "by taking away his ballet dancer. You have humiliated him and men dislike being humiliated. He is your enemy, always remember that."

"I will not forget it," the Marquis replied ominously.

"But I think it would be a good idea," Druscilla went on, "if we told your Grandmama – if we have to say where we met – that it was after I left the service of Lord and Lady Walden. That at least may serve to eliminate any mention of the Duke and Duchess."

"You think of everything," the Marquis agreed, "and, if I can do anything to level up with Walden, it will be a pleasure."

He bent forward and looked out as the horses slowed down.

"I think we have arrived," he murmured.

The Marquis escorted Druscilla into the inn. There was only a sleepy barkeeper to take their orders for breakfast and Druscilla went upstairs to tidy herself.

When she came down again into the small private sitting room where the Marquis had ordered the meal to be brought, she found him with a large glass of brandy in his hand staring sullenly at the newly-lit fire.

He looked up at her approach, but was not much cheered by her appearance.

She had taken off her bonnet, but her hair was still dragged back from her forehead in an unbecoming bun and her dress, cheap and ugly in the candlelight, looked even worse in the pale morning sunshine struggling through the diamond-paned windows.

She smiled at him and he noticed, as he had done in the schoolroom, that her eyes were a strange shade of green.

At the same time her gown made her skin seem sallow and there was no doubt that her whole appearance was drab to the point of ugliness.

After one glance the Marquis looked away from her, having an irrepressible desire to curse his wife or even strike her.

This was the woman he was married to, the Marchioness of Lynche, the woman his friends would be asked to believe had captured the most fastidious and sophisticated bachelor in the whole gay coterie of young bucks, who had attached themselves to the Prince Regent!

Had any man ever been trapped more neatly and completely?

*

Breakfast was served and they sat in silence.

It seemed as though they were both deep in their own thoughts and the Marquis drank a great deal of brandy.

Then they set off once again, this time the Marquis tooling his own high-perch phaeton.

They had covered quite a number of miles before Druscilla said,

"You drive well – I expected it."

"Damn it all!" the Marquis expostulated, "I am supposed to be a Corinthian."

"A lot of men call themselves that," Druscilla replied scornfully, "but it does not say that they can handle their horses as you are handling yours."

"1 am grateful for the compliment," he said sarcastically.

"I was stating a fact. I hope you will allow me my own curricle. Actually I drive rather well."

"I will try to find you something safe and quiet."

She smiled faintly but said nothing and there was little exchange between them until finally, when it was still only eight o'clock in the morning, the Marquis brought the phaeton to a standstill in front of a large porticoed house halfway down Curzon Street.

A surprised footman opened the door.

"Is her Ladyship awake?" the Marquis enquired. "Ask the Marchioness if she would be so gracious as to receive her grandson, the Marquis of Lynche."

"Yes, my Lord, of course, my Lord," the footman stammered, obviously put out by receiving callers at such an early hour.

Druscilla looked around her. The hall was large and imposing. There was a double staircase leading up towards the balustraded balcony overlooking it and a huge chandelier twinkled and glittered in the centre.

'What a house for a party,' she thought to herself.

But she said nothing as the Marquis fidgeted beside her, obviously tense and a little apprehensive of the interview that lay ahead of them.

The footman returned.

"Her Ladyship is breakfasting, my Lord. She will be delighted for your Lordship to join her."

The Marquis nodded and then looked at Druscilla.

"Come along," he urged her, "this is your idea."

"Yes, I know," Druscilla said and, although she was very pale, she gave no other sign of nervousness as they walked up the elegant staircase towards the breakfast room.

At the door, held open by a footman, Druscilla held back to let the Marquis go in first.

"Valdo, this is indeed a surprise!" she heard an old voice say, but a voice still with vitality and spirit about it. "What can have occurred that I should be honoured at such an early hour?"

The room was bathed in sunshine and, seated at a round table near the window, there was a very old lady, her face wrinkled and her hair very white against a parchment-coloured skin.

But the Dowager's eyes were bright and as piercing as a hawk's and she turned them upon Druscilla even as the Marquis bent to kiss her blue-lined hand.

"And who is your companion?" she asked. "Can this be the reason for your unexpected visit?"

"It is indeed, Grandmama, and perhaps you might remember her. Her name is 'Druscilla' and she happens to be your great-niece."

"Druscilla, poor Clementine's child!" the Dowager exclaimed. "I have often wondered what had happened to you."

She held out her hand and Druscilla dropped her a curtsey and kissed the old fingers even as the Marquis had done.

"You were a little girl when I last saw you," the Dowager went on. "I blame myself that we have lost touch all these years. But your father was a very difficult man. He made it clear that he had no desire to see me or to have anything further to do with me after your mother died."

"That was true, ma'am," Druscilla nodded. "But my father has been dead for nearly three years now."

"Then you are alone! You poor child. And that perhaps is why my grandson has brought you here."

Her eyes flickered over the cheap cotton dress and the ugly straw bonnet.

The Marquis then cleared his throat.

"Well, you see, Grandmama," he said, "Druscilla has been turned away from the house where she has been employed and I – "

"No, don't say that," Druscilla interrupted, "no, please."

The Marquis looked at her in perplexity and the Dowager with interest.

Then she turned to the Marquis,

"Would you be obliging enough – to go downstairs, Valdo? I want to talk to Great-Aunt Shermaline alone, I want to tell her the truth."

"But I thought you said – " the Marquis began.

"Your Grandmama must know the truth," Druscilla said quickly. "Now I have seen her I know that she is someone we cannot lie to and indeed it would be better if she knows but no one else."

The Marquis shrugged his shoulders.

"Very well, have it your own way."

He turned back towards the old lady.

"Have I your permission, Grandmama, to ask that I should be served with some wine in another room?"

"Chocolate or tea would be better for you," the Dowager pointed out with a little smile.

"I have no doubt of it," the Marquis replied, "but I have an insatiable desire for strong liquor at this particular moment. Druscilla will no doubt explain to you why."

He bowed conventionally and then, moving across the room, let himself out of the door.

The Dowager watched him go and then looked at Druscilla.

"You have certainly aroused my curiosity, child," she began. "You must have something very strange indeed to impart to me if it could bring my grandson calling on me before the world, his world, is properly awake, although I must admit that you both look as though you have been up all night."

"We have indeed," Druscilla answered.

The Dowager raised her eyebrows.

"In which case you are more in need of sustenance than my grandson."

She picked up a small bell from her side and rang it.

The door opened rapidly.

"Fresh chocolate for my visitor," the Dowager said, "and ask the chef to prepare some breakfast dishes immediately both for Miss Morley and for his Lordship, who is to be served downstairs."

"Very good, my Lady."

The door closed again and the Dowager held out her hand.

"Come and sit down, child. You look tired and a little apprehensive. I will not eat you, I promise you and perhaps I can help. I hope very much I can, I would like to do so."

Perhaps it was the kindness in the Dowager's voice that made Druscilla move forward impulsively and kneel beside the old lady's chair.

"Yes, you can help me," she said simply. "And please, Great-Aunt Shermaline, say you will, because it is of the utmost importance both to me and to – Valdo."

CHAPTER THREE

Sir Anthony Headley walked into the library at Lynche House and looked with astonishment at the Marquis sprawled in a chair with a glass of brandy in his hand and still wearing the clothes that he had driven back from Newmarket in.

"Good God, Valdo, you will be late!" Sir Anthony exclaimed. "And what the Devil is the meaning of this? You never said a word to me about it."

He held up a large card as he advanced across the room, looking the very Tulip of Fashion.

His elegant satin coat could only have been cut by a Master hand and his snowy-white cravat fell in intricate folds such as had indeed taken his valet over an hour to achieve.

The Marquis looked round at his friend with a jaundiced eye, glanced at the card and away again.

"So you have been invited," he said surlily. "I cannot conceive why."

"Cannot conceive why?" Sir Anthony repeated in astonishment. "Really, Valdo, that is doing it a bit brown! If I, as one of your oldest friends, was not to be present, then it is the outside of enough. Apart from that, why did you not mention to me something so momentous as your betrothal?"

There was a pause before the Marquis answered uncomfortably,

"It was a secret."

"But we drove back from Newmarket but two hours ago," Sir Anthony queried, "and you never gave me the slightest suspicion. Who is she? Why have I never heard of her before?"

"She is my cousin," the Marquis said briefly.

Sir Anthony eyed him speculatively. He and the Marquis had served together in the Army in Holland and he imagined that he knew his friend well, but this was a surprise that left him open-mouthed, but made him convinced that there was something strange about the whole circumstance.

"You are straining my credulity to the limit," he remarked drily, placing his invitation card in the inside pocket of his evening coat, "and, if you will pardon my mentioning it again, you are going to be unconscionably late."

The Marquis did not reply, but deliberately poured himself another brandy. The decanter was already half-empty and his friend watched him with a calculating expression on his face.

"You are not in trouble, are you, Valdo?" he asked at length. "Not being propelled to the altar in haste?"

There was no mistaking the innuendo behind his words and the Marquis replied angrily,

"No, no, nothing like that! I would have you know that I am not in the habit of playing about with unfledged wenches who don't know their dice."

"So I have always believed,' Sir Anthony said smoothly. "But why the secrecy?"

"Good God, Anthony, must I be responsible to you for everything I do?" the Marquis demanded.

"No, of course not," Sir Anthony replied. "But White's Club is in a tizzy and as for The Bachelors Club!"

"White's? The Bachelors?" the Marquis shouted. "What the *Hell* have they to do with it?"

"They have all been invited, dear boy, and surely you don't suppose that in your position, after all the loud-mouthed declarations you have made about the superior advantages of bachelorhood, that your *volte face* has not caused a sensation!"

"White's and The Bachelors'!" the Marquis muttered almost beneath his breath. "My grandmother must be insane!"

"It is a monumental occasion," Sir Anthony told him. "For God's sake, Valdo, you should be there now receiving your guests and not lounging about in your dirt."

His words seemed to rouse the Marquis from his lethargy. He poured the contents of the glass down his throat and went from the room, slamming the door behind him.

His friend gazed after him in consternation. That the Marquis should be about to embrace the bonds of Matrimony was one thing, but that he should be in such an ill temper about it was enough to make those who were fond of him exceedingly apprehensive.

Sir Anthony drew the invitation card from his pocket.

In black copperplate writing on a white card he read again,

"The Dowager Marchioness of Lynche has the honour to invite Sir Anthony Headley to a Reception prior to the announcement of the Marriage of her grandson, the Most Noble Marquis of Lynche, to Miss Druscilla Morley."

'Now who is Druscilla?' Sir Anthony asked himself.

It was over an hour later before he was to have the answer.

By that time the Marquis, exquisitely arrayed, had driven at his side to Curzon Street, where they found a *mêlée* of carriages and coaches blocking the street.

"You are unpleasantly late," Sir Anthony remarked, a statement that did nothing to relieve the scowl on the Marquis's face. "Why do we not walk?"

"I shall arrive in comfort," the Marquis snapped.

He glanced out of the window at the carriages waiting to disgorge their occupants at the great porticoed door of the Dowager's residence.

He recognised the Coats of Arms of most of them and thought with something like savagery that his grandmother was determined to make a fool of him.

There was no doubt that she had invited the whole of the *Bon Ton*, while he had imagined, when he had heard from her while he was at Newmarket, that what she intended was a small family gathering when he would introduce Druscilla to their joint relations.

This was something that he had not anticipated in his deepest despondency and he only wished that he had the courage to turn his horses round and tell Druscilla and all those who had come to smirk curiously at his choice of bride that they could all go to the Devil.

He knew only too well that the question he was going to be asked over and over again was 'why?'

Why had he chosen to espouse a girl, dull, unattractive, penniless and without position when every ambitious Mama in the whole Kingdom had been dangling after him since he had left Eton.

And what explanation could he make to those married beauties who he had been closely associated with and who had often loved him unwisely and far too well?

He had dallied with numbers of them and, if he had left some with an aching heart, he prided himself that they had at least remained his friends and that after the first partings were over they bore him no ill will.

But they would not be willing to be ousted from a place in his affections by some green girl with nothing to recommend her save the honour of being a rather distant cousin.

The whole aspect of what lay before him made the Marquis want to swear as he had sworn in Druscilla's presence when they had left the Duke's Castle.

He found himself clenching his hands together in an effort of self-control and he must have closed his eyes momentarily because, without his realising it, the horses had come to a standstill in front of the lit door and Sir Anthony was already stepping out of the coach onto the red carpet.

The Marquis followed him to find the marble hall filled to suffocation.

There was the flutter of silks, satins, velvets and gauze, the glitter of jewels and decorations, the heady fragrance of a hundred different perfumes and above all the high chatter of voices and laughter.

To the Marquis there seemed almost an obvious note of curiosity in the sound as though they were all asking each other,

"Why? Why is the perennial bachelor surrendering his much vaunted freedom?"

He stood almost bemused for a moment, not noticing provocative glances and the smiling lips turned towards him.

Then Sir Anthony touched his arm.

"You had best climb the other staircase," he suggested.

The two staircases ascended from the hall in a graceful arch and it was obvious that at the top of the left hand one the guests were being received, while the other was comparatively empty.

Obediently the Marquis walked up the right hand side, only slowing his steps as he approached the top to stare across the banks of flowers on the wide landing where he could see his grandmother, her white hair crowned with a glittering tiara, greeting the guests being stentoriously announced by a Major Domo in the Lynche livery.

"His Grace the Duke of Devonshire and Her Grace the Duchess."

"His Excellency the Ambassador of Russia and The Princess Lieven."

"The Viscount Newburton."

His voice was the voice of doom the Marquis felt.

Then he forced himself to look at the girl who stood at his grandmother's side.

For a moment he thought that it was a stranger! It was certainly someone he had never seen before. Or had he?

Then as he moved, as if under some compulsion, towards the head of the other staircase, he could hear his grandmother's voice ringing out clearly,

"I want you to meet my great-niece, Druscilla Morley, who is betrothed to my grandson. Druscilla – his Lordship is a very dear friend."

So it was Druscilla! The Marquis could hardly believe his eyes.

Druscilla, whom he had last seen in her hideous drab brown gown as any impoverished housemaid, was now transformed into someone he found it almost impossible to recognise.

The first thing he noticed was her hair. He remembered that it had always been red, but nothing like the living glowing red beloved by the Venetian painters, which now framed a little pointed face with the most enormous eyes he ever remembered seeing.

They were eyes that were undoubtedly green and which seemed to have a strange glittering brilliance that outshone even the emeralds in her hair and the magnificent necklace that encircled the rounded column of her neck.

The Marquis vaguely recalled the emeralds as being family jewels, which his mother had always felt were too spectacular for her to wear.

On Druscilla they looked sensational and he could see at first glance that she stood out in some extraordinary way even amongst the jittering throng of other bejewelled and beautiful women.

He was experienced enough in the female sex to realise that her gown was daring. No unmarried woman would have attempted to wear such a garment and indeed very few married ones.

Of emerald green it sparkled and glittered as if a thousand jewels were sewn over the thin gauze and it could not escape the eye of any man, no matter how old he might be.

The Marquis must have stood there staring in a bemused fashion for suddenly the Dowager looked up and saw him and held out her hand.

"Valdo, my dear grandson," she exclaimed, "how glad I am to see you!"

He stepped in front of the next guest waiting to be received and bent over her hand and then automatically found himself holding Druscilla's fingers in his.

"My Lord, we were worried about you," she said in a clear voice and then in a whisper that only he could hear she added sharply, "Make some plausible excuse for being late."

"I must apologise," the Marquis said obediently, "for not being here earlier, but there was an accident on the Newmarket road. A stagecoach had overturned. Was that not so, Anthony?"

Sir Anthony Headley, who was just behind the Marquis, stepped gallantly into the breach.

"Yes indeed, ma'am," he addressed the Dowager. "There was er – baggage and screaming females all over the road. We could not proceed until we had offered our assistance."

"How kind of you," Druscilla said, looking up at the Marquis with what appeared to be adoring eyes. "I do hope they were pretty."

There was a little giggle at this from those standing nearby.

"Well, now that you have arrived, Valdo," the Dowager told him sharply, "give Druscilla your arm and introduce her to your friends. Everyone is agog with curiosity to meet her."

Druscilla put the tips of her fingers on the Marquis's arm and he led her into the Reception Room where the tapers in the huge crystal chandeliers were fluttering a little in the breeze that came from the long French windows opening onto the garden at the back of the house.

The room was already half-full with guests who had arrived on time. At one end there was a champagne buffet with every sort of delicacy, all provided by the Dowager's excellent French chef, who was noted as being one of the best in London.

The Marquis was still too astonished at Druscilla's appearance to say little except to effect an introduction first to this person and then to another. To his astonishment his silence appeared unnoticed.

Druscilla talked gaily and charmingly and he realised now, beneath the light of the candles, that it was not only her gown but her skin that drew the eyes of everyone they spoke to.

Daringly revealed by the low-cut bodice of her gown, it was dazzlingly white, pure and unblemished as the petal of a camellia. Other women were rouged, Druscilla was not. There was only a slight touch of powder on her face.

But her mouth was invitingly red and there was no doubt that artifice had added to the original size and brilliance of her eyes.

They wandered from person to person and then quite unexpectedly the Marquis saw moving gracefully across the room towards them was the Duchess of Windleham.

He must have stiffened instinctively for Druscilla at once turned her head. But she was not as surprised as the Marquis since she had known even while she had protested at it that the Duke and Duchess had been sent an invitation.

"Don't be absurd, child," the Dowager had insisted. "For me to ignore them would be to cause comment and invite speculation. I shall send them a card and hope that they have the good sense to refuse."

Good sense was something that the Duchess had never had.

The Duke was not accompanying her, instead her hand was on the arm of a noble beau who still remained her devoted slave despite the fact that he had been replaced in her affections not once but a dozen times.

The Duchess was looking exceedingly lovely, Druscilla had to concede that. She was wearing a gown of pastel blue satin that showed off her fair hair and blue eyes to considerable advantage.

It also, Druscilla thought, made her look slightly older because it gave an impression of 'mutton dressed as lamb'. But that, she told herself, was only her opinion.

She felt sure that the Marquis was staring moonstruck at his lost love.

The Duchess came nearer and Druscilla saw her eyes narrow for a moment as they observed her Paris inspired gown and magnificent emerald jewellery.

Then with eyes that seemed almost to hold tears in them she stared up at the Marquis.

"Oh, my Lord," she cried in a voice that throbbed on the words, "I offer you all my good wishes for your happiness. I cannot tell you how much – it means to – me."

The Marquis bowed over her hand and then, as he realised that everyone around them was watching, he said with an effort,

"May I present my fiancée, Miss Druscilla Morley. Her Grace the Duchess of Windleham."

The Duchess did not extend her hand. She gave Druscilla the briefest nod and turned again to the Marquis.

"What a surprise," she said softly, "and where and when did you meet Miss er – Miss – this young – woman."

It was rude, it was insulting and those listening knew quite well that the Duchess had publicly declared herself to be unimpressed by the Marquis's intended.

It was well known where Her Grace's affections had lain for the past three months and the fact that she had captured the heart of the elusive Marquis of Lynche had been the subject of endless speculation.

"The first time I met Valdo," Druscilla stated clearly before the Marquis could speak, "was when I was in my cradle. He tried to take my bottle away from me!"

There was a ripple of laughter at this.

Druscilla waited for it to subside and then added,

"I believe he wanted the milk for his favourite guinea pig, but then Valdo has always had his favourites."

There was a little gasp and then the laughter rang out, The Duchess turned away, an expression of sheer fury on her face.

Druscilla sensed that the Marquis was rigid with anger, but she metaphorically shrugged her shoulders at his rage. If he would not protect her, she would protect herself.

From that moment there was no need for her to seek a champion. Her success was assured.

With a few words she had captivated the most critical and the most difficult audience in the world, the bored spoilt *Bon Ton* who wanted only to be relieved of their own boredom.

"Congratulations!"

It was not one of the Marquis's friends who said this with sincerity but all of them. Even the members of the Bachelors' Club told him that they would forgive him under the circumstances for defecting from their avowed bachelorhood.

"Extreme provocation is your excuse, eh, young man?" one of the older members asked, digging him in the ribs and looking at Druscilla with undisguised admiration. "Well, if I was younger, damme, but I should try to cut you out!"

It was nearly midnight when, preceded by the usual little buzz of Courtiers and toadies, the Prince Regent came into the Reception Room.

He was alone and had already made his apologies to the Dowager for the absence of Mrs. Fitzherbert, with whom he had been reunited, and for whom once again every social door was now open.

Yet it was not only Mrs. Fitzherbert's absence that had brought a frown to His Royal Highness's forehead and made him appear more pompous than usual.

Driving towards Curzon Street, Sir Anthony Headley had asked the Marquis,

"What about Prinny? He is not going to be pleased that you have not informed him of your matrimonial intentions."

The Marquis had not answered, but he had known that Sir Anthony spoke the truth. He was too close to the Prince Regent not to realise that His Royal Highness would consider such secrecy as an insult coming from one he had lavished his friendship on.

The Prince Regent spoke to two or three other people before the Marquis reached him and then, with a quite discernible note of peevish anger in his voice, he exclaimed,

"Why was I not told? You never mentioned anything of a betrothal to me."

It seemed to the Marquis as though the whole room held its breath waiting for his reply.

Then, before he could speak, Druscilla interceded.

Making the Prince Regent a very elegant curtsey, she looked up at him as she rose, her eyes in the light of the candles almost appearing to have the sparkle of fireworks in them.

"Pray don't be angry with poor Valdo, Sire, it was all my fault. I persuaded him, against his better judgment, into following Your Royal Highness's brilliant axiom when you said '*surprise is a most valuable weapon in battle*'."

"In battle?" the Prince Regent queried.

Druscilla dimpled at him.

"Yes, indeed, Sire, the battle to win Your Royal Highness's approval."

It was audacious and the Prince Regent liked it. He put back his head, laughed and then raised Druscilla's hand to his lips.

He could never resist flattery and, when it was flattery that concerned wars that he had never fought, but in which he considered himself an expert, he found it irresistible.

"May I take you down to supper, Miss Morley?" he asked. "I feel you must tell me more about the things I have said that have apparently aroused your interest."

"There will not be time to do that, Sire," Druscilla replied, unless you are prepared to stay for breakfast."

Again she had made him laugh and the Marquis stared after them as they proceeded down the room with a look of incredulity upon his countenance that only vanished when his grandmother pulled him sharply to attention for not having offered his arm to the Duchess of Devonshire.

From that moment it seemed to Druscilla that everything she said was greeted with laughter, not the sneering cynical laughter that the Marquis had dreaded, but laughter of genuine amusement and of flattering attention.

It was two o'clock in the morning before the Prince Regent finally withdrew from the Reception.

This was a great honour because it was unheard of for him to stay so late unless Mrs. Fitzherbert was present.

As he bid 'goodnight' to the Dowager Marchioness, he said,

"I have enjoyed the evening more than I deemed possible, ma'am. I am indeed delighted, although I had not expected to be, that your grandson and my friend is prepared at long last to embrace the state of Matrimony. May I suggest that if it was possible for him and this charming young lady to be wed before Mrs. Fitzherbert and I leave for Brighton, the Reception could be held at Carlton House."

"That is indeed an honour. Sire," the Dowager murmured.

"Will it be before that?" the Prince Regent asked, looking at Druscilla.

"Nothing but invasion by the French could prevent it, Sire." Druscilla smiled.

She felt his hand squeeze hers and then, with the Marquis in attendance and a dozen other cronies walking behind him, His Royal Highness descended the stairs to where his coach was waiting.

It was nearly two hours later that Druscilla and the Marquis found themselves alone.

The candles were guttering low and through the windows there was already a faint touch of gold in the sky and the stars were going out one by one.

Druscilla gave a little sigh.

"What a wonderful party!"

"How do you do it?" the Marquis asked.

It was the question that had been on his lips the whole evening and now at last, when they were alone and his grandmother had retired to bed, he could ask it.

Druscilla made no pretence of not understanding him,

"Hard work and prayer and, of course, your grandmother. She was fantastic and she appreciated, far better than anyone else could have done, how everything depended on my first appearance."

"But how could you look like this," the Marquis enquired, "when I remember – ?"

"Don't remember," she interrupted him swiftly, "don't let us think about it anymore. I am your cousin who has been living quietly in the country because of family mourning, but whom you have been seeing at regular intervals since you were a child. That is our story and we must not deviate from it."

She moved as she spoke and the Marquis caught a brief glimpse of her incredibly enticing figure beneath the thin gauze of her gown.

'Damn it, he thought, 'she might as well be naked,' and then he wondered if in fact she was.

"Tell me, Druscilla," he said aloud and then a voice broke in from the doorway,

"It cannot be true! I don't believe it!"

Standing theatrically with his arms held wide was an overdressed dandy. He was elegant almost to the point of femininity.

His fingers were adorned with rings, an enormous pearl and diamond tie-pin rested in his cravat, a fob hanging from his waistcoat onto his over-tight pantaloons was jewelled and it was difficult to imagine how he could have possibly squeezed into his green satin evening coat unless he had been stitched into it.

"Oh, it's you, Eustace," the Marquis said ungraciously.

"Yes, it is I, Eustace," was the reply, "and you might well be ashamed to see me. Only tell me, tell me, Valdo, this is not true! I cannot believe it is in you to crucify me."

"If you are referring to my engagement to Druscilla," the Marquis answered, "then it is most certainly true."

"Druscilla!" the newcomer exclaimed looking at her. "Do you mean to say that this is the Parson's brat from Lynche. I cannot credit it."

"Yes, I am the Parson's brat," Druscilla retorted. "and I remember you well, Cousin Eustace. You were always odious when I was a child and it does not appear that you have changed very much through the years. Last time we met you locked me in the potting shed so that I could not go fishing with Valdo when you wanted to be alone with him. As far as you are concerned, I might still be there."

Eustace Brent, only son of the previous Marquis of Lynche's younger brother, raised his looking glass to his eye and inspected Druscilla.

His face was painted, but no amount of cosmetics could hide the lines of dissipation, the dark shadows under his eyes or a general expression of querulousness resulting mainly, as the Marquis knew only too well, from the fact that his cousin was permanently in debt.

"Good God, it *is* Druscilla!" Eustace exclaimed at length. "Although I should be hard put to recognise you. But that is unimportant. What is of consequence is the fact that you appear to have forgotten, Valdo, that I am your heir."

"You have reminded me of it often enough," the Marquis commented wearily.

"And you have always told me that you would never marry. You reiterated over and over again that you were a confirmed bachelor," Eustace cried, his voice rising. "Can you imagine my feelings when on my return just tonight from the country I found an invitation from Grandmama?"

"I am sorry if it distressed you."

"Distressed me?" Eustace echoed. "I should have been here sooner to express not only my distress but my condemnation had it been that I did not immediately open my correspondence and it then took me some time to change my clothes."

"You are lucky to find us here," the Marquis said with a sigh. "I am just about to leave and Druscilla undoubtedly wishes to retire to bed."

"You shall not go until you have heard me out," Eustace insisted. "You must realise that you have put me in an impossible position."

"I cannot see why," the Marquis declared.

"But you have told me that you would never marry!" Eustace almost screamed. "You formed The Bachelor Club and everyone knew that you were the untouchable bachelor, the man every match-making mother despaired of."

"I have changed my mind," the Marquis admitted simply.

"I am afraid it is impossible for you to do so," Eustace said firmly.

"If you are trying to tell me that your pockets are to let once again and the duns are after you, very well, I will settle up. But this is the last time, Eustace. You have battened on me for too long."

"Too long?" his cousin asserted. "When I expected to be your heir?"

"My dear boy, face facts," the Marquis retorted. "I did not intend to marry, but you know as well as I do that the ideas one blabbers about when one is young can easily be changed. Druscilla and I will be married within the next three weeks, the Prince Regent has offered us a Reception at Carlton House. There is no more argument about it. Send me your bills and my secretary will see that they are met."

"I will not allow you to wed, I tell you, *I will not allow it*," Eustace shouted, stamping his foot.

Druscilla suddenly burst out laughing.

"Oh, Cousin Eustace, you have not changed in the slightest. I remember you behaving just like that when Valdo's father said that you could not drive his bays. You sulked for two days because he alleged that you were not experienced enough to handle them."

"Will you shut up," Eustace exploded rudely, "this does not concern you, Druscilla. I cannot think how you managed to entice Valdo into your toils, but I can assure you I will try to extract him from them. Marry someone else, anyone else, but not Valdo!"

"Eustace, you are in your cups," the Marquis said sharply. "I did not realise it when you arrived, but now I am sure that you are foxed and don't realise what you are saying. Go to bed, my dear fellow, I will talk to you tomorrow. At the moment you are being very irresponsible and not very polite to the future Marchioness."

His words seemed to make Eustace Brent pull himself together and instead of the rather hysterical tones charged with passion in the way he had been speaking, there was now a nasty sneering note in his voice, which seemed to Druscilla to have something evil about it.

"You will be sorry for this, Valdo," he warned, "and so will you, Druscilla. You cannot nudge me off in such a manner, not without taking the consequences."

He turned round as he spoke and walked quickly from the room. They heard him moving along the landing and down the stairs.

Druscilla turned to the Marquis in astonishment.

"Is he mad?" she asked.

"No more than usual," the Marquis replied. "He has always been a bit cock-brained about being my heir. I suspect that he has borrowed large sums already on the chance of his inheritance. Well, I will pay up as I have done before, but I am not going on doing it."

"I should think not," Druscilla agreed. "I have never liked Eustace and I remember now how possessive he was about you. He hated you to have any other friends. I think I realised that even though I was but a child."

"He is not an engaging person I am afraid, but don't let's trouble our heads over him."

"I have a feeling he is going to be very unpleasant," Druscilla said reflectively.

"What can Eustace do?" the Marquis asked, shrugging his shoulders. "I don't say that he would not serve us a backhander if he had the chance, but one thing he cannot do is stop the marriage, it is too late for that."

"No, he cannot," Druscilla concurred, "but I think he means to do something horrid to hurt you and he might even be dangerous."

"You are being nonsensical," the Marquis stated firmly. "Go to bed and dream about your triumph for damn it all, Druscilla, that is what it has been. A triumph and I never expected it!"

"You are – pleased?"

The question was simple and yet he felt that there was a hint of anxiety in her green eyes.

For a moment he hesitated and then he told her the truth.

"'Relieved' is the right word," he answered. "I never anticipated that you would look as you do or be so amusing and witty. How did you manage it, Druscilla? How the Devil did you manage, after the life you have led, to behave as you did tonight?"

Druscilla walked away from him towards the open window. By now the stars had gone and the sky bore the soft yellow of the dawn.

"Do you want to know the truth? Does – it really interest you?" she asked softly.

"To be honest, I am seriously curious," the Marquis admitted.

"Then I will tell you. As I began to grow up, you were no longer at Lynche Hall and there was little for me to do except read. I read and read, the Classics, history and biography, everything I could find and so I had some idea of what the world was like beyond the confines of a small English village. Then I started to tell myself – stories."

She paused and continued slowly,

"When I went out to work in those grand houses where I was incarcerated in the schoolroom, I learnt from the servants, as you so rightly gathered, what was happening in the social world downstairs. I began to imagine myself taking my place among the ladies and gentlemen. I thought of what I would say and how I would be amusing and interesting and not just as so many women are, a pretty face beneath an empty attic!"

"Well, tonight it certainly bore fruit, I wish my own education had been half as successful."

She flashed a sudden smile.

"That is generous of you. I know what you must have been feeling as you came here. That was why you were late, was it not?"

The Marquis found himself smiling down at her. There was a dimple in each of her cheeks he noticed and she had rather an amusing way of looking up at a man through her eyelashes. There was no doubt that she would be a great success.

"You have certainly taken your first fence in style," he said. "As for being generous, Druscilla, I think once again I owe you an apology."

"You need not make it," she answered. "Don't forget this is what I wanted. To me it is all exciting and a thrill beyond expression."

"I forgot," he murmured, "the 'adventuress' and audacious at that!"

"Exactly."

He laughed and raised her hand to his lips.

"Goodnight," he said, "and tell Grandmama I will call in the morning to thank her."

"Not too early," Druscilla suggested, "and don't forget that you are already seeing Eustace."

"Oh, *damn* Eustace. He is a cursed nuisance and always has been."

The Marquis walked down the stairs to where his coach with its attendants was still waiting for him.

Druscilla watched him go.

She had learnt a great deal about the Marquis these last weeks. He was not only a handsome, spoilt young man but a Corinthian who was admired by all his contemporaries, a good judge of horseflesh and an excellent rider.

And besides this the Dowager had told her that he had done extremely well in the Army.

"General Sir Ralph Abercromby, under whose command he served against the Dutch in the Helder Campaign," she told Druscilla, "told me himself with his own lips that there was no one he would rather have in a tight corner in command of men than Valdo and Sir Ralph, I can assure you, does not pay compliments easily."

Druscilla smiled at herself.

They had both been in a tight corner this evening. But it had not been Valdo who had found the way out but herself.

She caught sight of her reflections in one of the gilt mirrors and suddenly flung out her arms as if to embrace the world.

"It *is* exciting," she whispered aloud, "madly, wildly, deliriously exciting."

CHAPTER FOUR

The sun was sparkling on the horses' silver bridles as the Marquis tooled his tandem skilfully through the East gate into Hyde Park.

Druscilla felt that she had never been so happy.

She was well aware that there had been admiration in the Marquis's eyes when he collected her from his grandmother's house, having sent a footman with a note early in the morning to suggest that he should take her driving.

"What shall I – wear?" had been the inevitable feminine question that had come to her lips the moment she received the invitation.

The Dowager smiled.

"You have them talking and you have to keep them at it!"

In answer Druscilla had suddenly gone down on her knees beside the old lady's chair and taken one of her old blue-veined hands in both hers.

"How can I ever – thank you for last night?"

"By continuing to be the success that you undoubtedly were," the Dowager replied. "You have made a splash in the pool, keep the ripples going."

Druscilla had spoken a little unsteadily, but now she laughed, kissed the Dowager's hand and rose to her feet.

"Do you really credit it that they are talking about me – today?" she asked in a very young voice.

"They will be talking of nothing else," the Dowager promised her. "They have been speculating, questioning and anticipating what Valdo's future bride would be like. Now they know and, if it is not an unpleasant surprise to a large number of the so-called Society beauties, then I am no judge of my own sex."

"They hate me for – capturing him?" Druscilla asked.

"They will envy you and hope to destroy you," the Dowager answered. "And there is only one person who can let them do that and that is *you*."

"Then I must survive," Druscilla laughed. "And so I ask you again, cleverest of all the great-aunts in the world – what shall I wear?"

She had known that the Dowager's choice had been successful when she saw the Marquis's face. But now, as they turned into the Park and he lifted his tall hat from his head again and again to passing acquaintances, she knew that, while the men's eyes widened a little at the sight of her, the women's narrowed.

Her dress was simple enough, but clung to her figure and was almost transparent in the approved fashion set in Paris by Josephine, the wife of Napoleon Bonaparte.

Cut by a Master hand, it was of pale daffodil-yellow muslin, which seemed to have captured the very sunshine itself and in some strange way accentuated the camellia-white of her skin and gave an added fiery glint to her red hair.

Her high-brimmed bonnet was trimmed with ostrich feathers, which matched the topaz necklace that the Dowager had lent her to wear round her slim neck and there was a bracelet of the same glittering stones to encircle her tiny wrist.

"Did you enjoy yourself in Newmarket?" Druscilla asked the Marquis when they had driven for some way without speaking.

"The racing was disappointing and I lost money. Perhaps I was not in a winning mood."

"I have always heard that Newmarket is liable to produce slow horses and fast ladybirds," Druscilla observed.

The Marquis was so astonished at her remark that for a moment he loosened his hold on his team.

"Druscilla!" he exclaimed. "You are not to say such things."

"Who is to hear me save your chestnuts?" she asked. "And I will wager that they have heard a great deal worse on other occasions."

The Marquis's lips twitched at the corners and then he said,

"I beg of you to guard your tongue. I see Lady Jersey ahead and I will introduce you. But one word out of place and she could get you barred from Almacks. Then as far as your Social world is concerned, it would indeed be the end of the road."

"I will behave," Druscilla promised him with what was suspiciously like a little giggle.

The Marquis drew up his team beside an open carriage where sat the uncrowned Queen of Society and the most redoubtable woman in England.

Vivacious as a hummingbird, she nevertheless could be as cruel as a panther and as dangerous as an adder to anyone who incurred her displeasure.

But it was with a smile of genuine affection that she greeted the Marquis.

"I am indeed piqued that I missed your grandmother's party last night, Valdo," she began.

"There was only one thing wrong with it – you were not there," the Marquis replied gallantly.

Lady Jersey's eyes were taking in every detail of Druscilla's appearance.

"You may present your fiancée," she said as if it was a Royal command.

"This is my second cousin, Druscilla Morley, ma'am,' the Marquis smiled. "She is, as you know, staying with my grandmother until our Wedding."

Lady Jersey gave Druscilla a brief nod.

"I have already heard," she said, turning once again to the Marquis, "you are to have your Reception at Carlton House. You must indeed be in favour."

"If I am it must be because you have always been so kind about me."

Lady Jersey gave a little laugh.

"You were always a very skilful flatterer, my dear Valdo. It is an unusual quality in an Englishman because most of them cannot string two pleasant words together."

"I have never flattered you," the Marquis replied. "I have been but truthful."

For a moment the vivaciousness of Lady Jersey seemed to still. She looked up at the Marquis and there was something in her eyes that made Druscilla purse her lips.

Then the Marquis swept his hat from his head and they were driving down Rotten Row, the horses joining the train of other vehicles, polished and blazoned with crests and Coats of Arms each smarter and more elegant than the last.

"Is Lady Jersey one of your flirts?" Druscilla enquired.

"That is not the sort of question you should ask," the Marquis answered reprovingly. "Really, Druscilla, you must try to behave in a more circumspect manner."

Druscilla sighed.

"Oh dear, I can see how unexceptionable our conversations will be in the future."

She smiled as she continued,

"'Good morning, my Lord, I shall say. I hope you slept well. Passably, you will reply.'

"'I have a suspicion that your Lordship was somewhat late in returning home or was I mistaken?'

"'I became involved,' you undoubtedly will answer, 'in a somewhat ponderous discussion on the possibility of Bonaparte's Amnesty being but a pretence to give him time to build an invasion fleet.'

"'How fascinating, my Lord! And did this exchange of ideas take place in the White House or at Mrs. Barclay's'?"

"Druscilla!"

The Marquis was so startled at Druscilla mentioning the two most notorious bawdy houses in London that once again his horses leapt forward and he had some difficulty in controlling them.

"Where the Devil did you hear of such places?" he asked. "Let alone to speak of them?"

Druscilla did not answer and after a moment he looked down at her and said,

"Dammit, I believe you are deliberately trying to provoke me. You tell me you were spanked as a child. All I can say is it was not often or hard enough."

Druscilla bent her head.

"I see I must retrieve your cricket bat for you, my Lord," she said in a meek voice.

The Marquis's lips twitched and then suddenly he laughed and Druscilla was laughing with him.

"You are very gay, Valdo," Sir Anthony Headley exclaimed, drawing up beside him.

He was riding a spirited stallion, which showed off his neat figure and elegantly cut riding coat to considerable advantage. Druscilla also liked the rakish angle at which he wore his high conical hat.

"Good morning, Sir Anthony," she greeted him.

"Your servant. Miss Morley. May I thank you for a very enjoyable party yestereve."

"You must thank Valdo's grandmother," Druscilla replied. "I enjoyed it more than I have ever enjoyed an evening in the whole of my life."

There was something infectious in her enthusiasm.

"Shall I see you tonight at Lady Lansdown's?" Sir Anthony enquired.

The Marquis groaned.

"Don't tell me I have to endure another of those stiff social functions?" he asked. "One is enough."

"Of course you need not come if it bores you," Druscilla said quickly. "Sir Anthony, would you be kind enough to escort me? My great-aunt is giving a small dinner party before the ball."

"I should be most honoured to do so – " Sir Anthony replied, only to have his words cut short by the Marquis.

"Thank you, Anthony, but I am perfectly capable of escorting my own fiancée even if she wishes to spend an evening of unthinkable boredom."

"But, of course, you have a prior claim," Sir Anthony said suavely, "in which case I will see you both at the Lansdowns. Until then, Miss Morley, and I hope you will save me at least one dance."

"You shall have one as soon as I arrive," Druscilla promised him.

Her words were cut short by the fact that the Marquis whipped up his horses and drove off.

"It's no use making sheep's eyes at Anthony," he told her sharply.

"I did not want you to inconvenience yourself," she answered gently. "You are so used to these functions, but they are new and fascinating to me."

"'Inconvenience' is the right word," the Marquis went on. "But if it has to be done, it has to be done. Thank God there are only a few weeks left before the Prince Regent leaves London and then the Season will be over."

"And where will we go then?" Druscilla asked.

"I have not yet determined what we shall do after the Wedding," the Marquis replied crushingly.

She knew that he was annoyed again by the way he pushed his horses and thrust out his jaw, which she remembered him doing as a boy.

They drove some way in silence and then she said coaxingly,

"Please don't be cross, Valdo. What has happened – has happened. No amount of disagreeableness will undo it now."

"No, you are right," the Marquis nodded. "I just don't want to see you make a cake of yourself."

"I think the truth is," Druscilla replied, "that we are making a cake of everyone else. Only we know the truth and it is quite amusing to watch them being taken in."

She realised that she had struck the right note when she saw the Marquis smiling again.

"God! They would be mad as fire if they knew what we were about! And the only one who could tell them would be – "

He was about to say 'the Duchess', but then he changed his mind.

"There is no chance of anyone betraying us," Druscilla said quietly, but even as she spoke she thought that she was boasting and superstitiously crossed her fingers.

'It has to be kept a secret, it must be,' she told herself and found herself praying.

Nothing must spoil her incredible happiness.

*

There were innumerable invitations to be answered during the afternoon and the Dowager insisted that Druscilla should lie down for a short while before robing herself for Lady Lansdown's ball.

Druscilla protested that she was too excited to rest, but when the time came she fell asleep for nearly an hour, only to dream that she was back in a dark and gloomy schoolroom and filled with a sudden inexpressible terror because someone was turning the handle of the locked door.

She woke with a scream to find that her heart was pounding.

She had been re-living the panic-stricken fears that had haunted her for so long that she could not believe that they were over now.

For a moment she lay on the soft curtain-draped bed and thought that she must still be dreaming and then she realised where she was and experienced a relief beyond all words.

For the first time in her life she was safe.

She was married – married to a man who, even if he was unwillingly her husband, was nevertheless legally her protector.

Never again need she be frightened of starvation or worse still of having to submit to the advances of men she loathed and despised and never again need she know the same fear that had woken her now, fear that made her mouth dry and her whole body so weak that she was almost paralysed by the very terror of it.

'I am safe! *I am safe!*'

She repeated the words to herself over and over again until finally she believed them and slipped from her bed to stand staring into the mirror on her dressing table.

Could this really be Druscilla, that miserable terrified girl who had deliberately made herself look drab and unattractive?

Could this be the same girl who at times had thought despairingly that death was preferable to life or that the only hope of being left unmolested was to grow so old and ugly that men would turn away from her in disgust?

And yet the mirror told her all too dearly what the men had been perceptive enough to see beneath the disguise that she had attempted to deceive them with.

Her skin, the soft almost immature curves of her small breasts, her tiny heart-shaped face, her enormous green eyes and above all the glowing richness of her red hair tumbling over her shoulders and falling in silken waves well below her waist.

Just for a moment Druscilla stared at herself and then turned away. Even now she was still afraid of her own attractions.

For too long they had been something that she had feared almost to the point of loathing because when men looked at her they turned into swine.

But there was no sign of anything else except youth and excitement in her face when she came down to dinner.

Once again there had been a question to her great-aunt of what she should wear and the Dowager had counselled her wisely.

"Surprise them," she advised. "Last night you were sophisticated, almost outrageous. You looked not a young untouched girl but a woman of the world, the only sort of female they would expect to capture and enslave a man as elusive as 'the Bachelor Marquis'. Tonight be young and simple rather than exotic, charm them rather than entice. They will not know what to expect when they see you again."

"Oh, you are so wise," Druscilla exclaimed. "Shall I ever be as perceptive and clever as you?"

"Only when you are as old as I am," the Dowager replied cynically, "and then it will not matter what you wear!"

So Druscilla had chosen a dress of white Parisian gauze with only a few small turquoises embroidered round the hem. These were echoed by the turquoise ribbons that crossed her breasts and hung in a girlish bow down her back.

There were turquoise slippers peeping beneath the hem of her dress and turquoise satin bows instead of bracelets were tied at her wrists to hold her white gloves in place.

"How do I look?" Druscilla asked when she went to the Dowager's bedroom before going downstairs.

"As young as spring until they look into your eyes," the old lady replied.

Druscilla laughed.

"You mean there is a devil lurking in them somewhere?"

"Exactly," the Dowager smiled, "and that is why they will not find you a milksop however you affect them in other ways."

But, as she walked downstairs, Druscilla was thinking of her effect on only one person – the Marquis.

He was waiting in the salon where they were to congregate before dinner and surprisingly he was on time before the rest of the guests arrived.

He looked up at her as she approached and set down the brandy glass he held in his hand. He watched her walk across the room towards him and once again he noticed the enticement of her exquisite figure and the way her hair glinted in the light of the candles.

"It is good of you to be on time," Druscilla said as she curtseyed to him. "Your grandmama is relying on you to play host at dinner."

His eyes seemed to take in every detail of her appearance and she guessed that he was well versed in women's gowns.

"No jewellery?" he asked after a moment.

"A change from last night. Would you rather I put some on? There is enough in all conscience to choose from."

"No, stay as you are, but I hope one day you will wear the diamonds I can remember my mother looking like a Fairy Princess in when she came to kiss me goodnight before she went to Court."

"I have seen the Lynche diamonds," Druscilla replied, "and they are magnificent. But I think perhaps they should wait until I am officially married."

"Perhaps that would be best," the Marquis agreed.

Druscilla suddenly realised that what they were saying aloud had little or nothing to do with what they were thinking.

She was not quite sure of the Marquis's thoughts, but she, herself was almost tinglingly aware of the closeness of him and the fact that he was in some way a very different person from the boy she had always remembered.

The boy she had thought of so often during those years when they had been apart.

It was not only what his grandmother had said of him and it was not only the admiration that he commanded from other women or the way they looked at him.

To her he was a man and the feeling was so strong that she drew back a little from him suddenly afraid and suddenly apprehensive.

Then he smiled and she found herself smiling back at him.

"So tonight is another adventure," he said and there was so much charm about him that she found herself irresistibly drawn back to his side.

"Of course," she answered. "Who knows what will happen. Although indeed after captivating the Prince Regent last night, there is no one more important left, unless we are visited by the Archangel Gabriel himself!"

The Marquis was laughing as the guests arrived and it turned out to be a very lively dinner party. The Dowager's dry cynical wit and Druscilla's unpredictable remarks made the guests exclaim almost ruefully when it was time to leave for the ball.

"Bachelorhood! Who wants to be a bachelor?" Druscilla heard one of the older men exclaim as he slapped the Marquis on the back. "You are a fortunate young fellow, although I expect everyone tells you that."

"Yes, indeed," the Marquis replied and just for a moment Druscilla wondered if he resented her being such a success.

The ball was a huge crush and the Dowager's party had to wait for nearly half an hour on the stairs before they could reach the ballroom.

Having once lost one's party it would have been almost impossible to find them again and Druscilla began to understand why the Marquis should find such squeezes a bore.

When, long after midnight, she returned from dancing with Sir Anthony Headley, it was to discover that the Dowager had gone home, leaving a message that, as there were so many more parties to attend, Druscilla was not to stay late.

"I am ready to leave now," she told the Marquis.

"You are? Well, Heaven be praised for that! There is no need to make your farewells, let us slip away while we have the opportunity."

"I think that would be best," Druscilla agreed.

She put out her hand to Sir Anthony.

"Goodnight and thank you. I enjoyed our dance, even though we could hardly move."

"I enjoyed it more than I can say," he replied and raised her fingers to his lips despite the fact that the Marquis glared at him.

"I cannot think what has got into Anthony," he grumbled as he went down the stairs with Druscilla, "prancing about like one of those smarmy frogs across the Channel."

Druscilla did not answer and indeed the Marquis did not seem to expect her to do so. As soon as the carriage was called, he hurried her into it and then to her surprise she heard him tell the footman to drive to Lynche House.

"I have just remembered," he said as they set off that I bought a present for Grandmama today, a trifling gift for all she has done for you. I meant to bring it with me tonight, but I forgot. Perhaps you would tell the servants to put it on her breakfast tray. It will surprise her when she wakes."

"How kind of you!" Druscilla cried. "She will be thrilled, I know she will. She so often wondered if you would approve of what we are doing."

"Approve, of course I approve. There are very few women of her age who would come up to scratch at a moment like this."

"There is no one like her," Druscilla agreed with warmth in her voice. "She is wonderful, she is really. She has entered into the whole spirit of the plot. We could never have done any of this without her."

"No, indeed, that is why I have bought her something that I am sure she will like."

"I wish you could have given it to her tonight," Druscilla said and then added, "No, perhaps it is better as it is. She can open it alone and nobody will be surprised at your giving her something so valuable – if it is?"

"It was very expensive if that is what you are trying to say and I assure you it is something she will like."

"Tell me what it is."

"No," he answered, "I would like to surprise you too. Incidentally there are two presents."

"Two?" Druscilla asked. "Not – not one for me as well?"

"Yes, one for you too."

"Then I cannot wait for the morning to see it," Druscilla cried, "I shall open it the moment you give it to me."

"Very well," he said, amused by her excitement. "I will not keep you long. I have put my gifts in the safe and only I have the key, so I shall have to fetch them myself. Stay in the coach until I return. It would not be conformable for you to enter the house of your *fiancé* at this hour of the night!"

He accentuated the word fiancé and Druscilla giggled.

"If people only knew."

"Thank God they don't," the Marquis said sharply.

A footman opened the door of the coach and the Marquis went into the house.

Druscilla sat waiting. The lights from the hall cast a gleam across the pavement and she could see part of a carved gilt table with a mirror above it.

'Soon I shall be living here!' she thought and felt an odd sensation, which she could not translate into words even to herself.

It was then she noticed that a man roughly dressed had come to the door of the house and was speaking to the footman on duty.

"Be that Lord Lynche who I sees goin' in?" he asked.

"Yes, that was his Lordship," the footman replied.

"Then give 'im this 'ere note. Give it into 'is own hand, do you savvy? No one else is to see it, it be from 'Er Grace."

The man dropped his voice at the last word, but Druscilla heard it distinctly. She saw the man, whoever he might be, press a coin into the footman's and then he turned and disappeared into the shadows.

Impulsively, without even considering what she was doing, Druscilla stepped out of the coach. She walked into the doorway after the footman, who had taken but a few steps back into the hall.

"Give me that note," she ordered him authoritatively.

"It be for his Lordship, miss," the footman responded.

"I will give it to him," Druscilla said and took it from the man.

The servant stared at her in surprise as she opened the piece of paper, which was held together by a wafer.

There were only a few words written on it,

"I must see you immediately, I am desperate!
My coach is waiting on the other side of the square.
C."

Druscilla read the words twice and then she slipped the note down the front of her dress and turned to walk back to the coach.

'*Damn her!*' she cursed to herself furiously. 'She cannot leave him alone! She will spoil everything. The Duke will find out and – there will be a scandal. I will not allow it. I will stop her – if it is the last thing I do.'

She looked across the square and through the trees and shrubs in the garden she thought she could see on the far side the dark outline of a coach.

She stood staring at it for a moment and then on an impulse pulled her cloak around her and sped across the gardens. She felt her slippers sink into the soft earth as she pushed her way through the lilac bushes and out the other side.

She had been right. There was the closed carriage drawn by only one horse.

There was no doubt, Druscilla thought, that the Duchess must be inside, waiting for the Marquis, waiting to make more trouble than she had made already.

Druscilla ran to the door of the coach and pulled it open.

"I want to speak to your Gr – " she began and then suddenly was caught by rough hands that dragged her inside.

Before she could cry out and before she even realised what was happening, a sack was pulled over her head and she felt herself being thrown violently onto the back seat and the carriage started off.

For a moment she did not scream, she was too taken by surprise, besides the sack itself was suffocating and the rough way that she had been thrown into the corner had almost knocked the breath out of her body.

Then, as she opened her mouth to cry out for help, a rough harsh voice beside her exclaimed,

"This ain't a man, this be a fancy mort. 'E said as 'ow it'd be a Lord."

"I knows," another man replied, "and 'e says if 'is Lordship struggles to konk 'im one on the 'ead. What we do now 'tis a female?"

"Help!" Druscilla managed to cry. "Help! There has been – some mistake."

Her voice sounded weak and far away through the confines of the sack.

"Shall I 'it 'er?" one of the men asked and suddenly she was silent.

"I don't know. 'Er be very small, you might kill 'er," the other man answered.

Druscilla could feel the closeness of his body and suddenly she realised the appalling danger that she was in and fell silent.

"'Er ain't a-strugglin' now," the first man said, "perhaps she's fainted."

"'Er can't be dead?" the other man asked in frightened tones. "You were rough. I weren't expectin' no female."

"I were expectin' the swell 'e says would come."

"So was I."

"Do you think we've got the wrong person?"

There was silence.

"We'd best ask," the first man said, "and if 'ave to konk 'er, I'll konk 'er gentle-like."

"Shall I take the sack off 'er?" the other man asked.

"No, no, let's leave 'er as she be. 'E'll know what to do."

Druscilla felt the man beside her rise. He must have put his head out of the window because she heard him shout to the coachman,

"'Ere, Charlie go back to 'is Nibs!"

Druscilla kept still. It was very hot and airless inside the sack and pulled down almost to her wrists it made her effectively captive. Any struggle she might make she knew would be to no avail.

Besides she was afraid of being 'konked' and had a sudden fear that the man would hit her face and not her head.

The coach rumbled on for a short way. The going was smooth and wherever 'his Nibs' lived, Druscilla felt that it must be in the best part of the City.

Finally they came to a standstill.

"Shall I fetch 'im?" one of the men asked.

"You 'ad best go and tell 'im what's 'appened. We daren't take the fancy mort to the river till we knows if it be the right one to drown."

As the man scrambled out of the coach, Druscilla heard a voice that she recognised all too clearly.

"What the hell are you doing back here? You cannot have disposed of him already."

"No, sir, it be like this, sir. It weren't a-like you says who comes to the coach, but a female."

"A female? What do you mean, a female?"

Druscilla could hear the usual high note of querulousness in Eustace's voice when he was cross or upset.

"Like I says, sir, a fancy mort comes to the door and we pulls 'er in afore we realises who 'er be."

"Fools! Dopes! Can I trust no one to do anything! Here, let me have a look."

Druscilla could hear the footsteps approaching the coach and then she was conscious that Eustace was about to peer into the darkness inside.

"'Er 'as either fainted or 'er be dead, sir," the other man who had remained in the coach now piped up.

"Dead? Did you hit her?"

"No, sir, just handled 'er a bit rough when we puts the sack over 'er 'ead."

There was a moment's silence while Druscilla waited, hardly daring to breathe.

"Shall we put 'er in the river?" the first man asked almost timidly.

"You idiots, you stupid bungling fools! Take her back!" Eustace almost screamed. "Take her back to where you found her. Put her down in Berkeley Square and leave her there. They will imagine it was footpads who assaulted her."

"And what about the gentleman, sir?"

"Forget him, you have done enough damage for tonight."

"And our gold?"

"Gold, what gold do you deserve? I will pay you half what I promised you and not a penny more. But you don't deserve it after messing up the job."

"It ain't our fault!"

"Then whose is it, you numbskulls? Come back when you have set her down again and on foot, mark you. I don't want carriages driving up here at all hours of the night. On foot do you understand?"

"Yes, sir."

"And if you are not quick about it I will give you nothing. Blundering, miserable turnip-heads! I cannot trust one of you to do the simplest job."

There was the sound of feet going up some steps and then the slam of a door.

The man who had been outside the coach climbed in again. The coachman whipped up his horse and Druscilla realised that they were driving back the way they had come.

"'E said as 'ow they'd think it were footpads," the man who had remained in the coach said. "Shall I look to see if 'er 'as any sparklers?"

"No, leave 'er be," the other man asserted angrily. "We're the ones who'll be on Tyburn if 'er be dead, not 'is Nibs. 'E'll say as 'ow 'e's never seen us afore, you knows that as well as I do."

"If we takes 'er back perhaps they'll be waitin, to catch us," the man with the frightened voice said and Druscilla felt that he was the younger of the two.

"We'll do as we be told, 'e won't pay us otherwise. Any excuse and 'e'll keep the money. Only 'alf is what we gets anyway."

The man lapsed into silence.

Druscilla kept very still. It was getting harder and harder to breathe in the sack. Finally, when she felt as though she was suffocating and drifting into unconsciousness, the coach came to a standstill.

"There be people about," the younger man said apprehensively.

"Well, 'urry," the elder one replied. "Get 'er out quick and chuck 'er in the grass."

Even now Druscilla was not certain that they would not hit her, so she was careful to remain completely limp as she felt herself being bundled very roughly out of the coach.

The two men then swung her and, as she struggled to save herself, she felt the sudden hard impact of the ground.

She had no idea how long she was unconscious, but she was suddenly aware that the sack had been pulled off her face and there were a number of people staring down at her.

She opened her eyes and drew in a deep breath of air.

She could see vaguely some indistinguishable figures and above them the tall trees silhouetted against the sky.

Then she heard the Marquis's voice,

"What is it? What have you found?"

"Valdo," she tried to cry out and found that her voice died in her throat.

"The young lady is here, my Lord," she heard someone saying, "she was thrown out of the coach a few minutes ago. I saw them do it myself while we were searching the bushes."

As she closed her eyes in relief that she was safe, Druscilla felt herself as easily as if she was a child in the Marquis's arms.

He carried her through the garden, across the pavement and in through the door of Lynche House.

"Bring some wine immediately," he commanded as they reached the hall and he carried her into a room alight with candles.

He set her down on the sofa. As he did so, she gave a little cry, realising for the first time that, when the men had thrown her onto the ground, they had bruised her back.

"It's all right," the Marquis said soothingly, "you are safe."

He left her a moment to take a glass of wine that the butler poured out for him.

"Drink this if you can," he urged her quietly, going down on one knee beside her and lifting the glass to her lips.

She took a sip and then pushed her hair back from her forehead.

"I – am – all right," she murmured uncertainly.

The Marquis glanced at the butler.

"Keep the coach, Bateman, I will take Miss Morley home as soon as she is well enough to travel."

"Very good, my Lord."

The butler withdrew and Druscilla heard the door close behind him. Then with an effort she pulled herself up against the silk cushions.

"It was – Eustace!" she stammered.

"I somehow guessed it," the Marquis replied. "Are you all right?"

"A little – bruised. They thought – I was unconscious – otherwise they would have – hit me."

"Where were they taking you?" he asked.

"They thought it was you they had captured. They were going – to drown – you."

"Good God!"

There was no doubt that the Marquis was profoundly shocked.

"I cannot believe it," he said, moving away from her towards the fireplace. "Would Eustace really go to such lengths to inherit? It just cannot be true."

"It is – true," Druscilla murmured.

She was suddenly aware that her hair was hanging untidily over her shoulders and with an effort raised her arms to pin it into some semblance of order,

"I knew he was half-mad," the Marquis remarked, "but not mad enough to commit murder."

Druscilla rose a little unsteadily to her feet.

"It was fortunate that I went to the coach – in your place. From the way the men talked, they seemed utterly ruthless and – were prepared to do anything for money. When they had battered you unconscious, they would have dumped you in the Thames and then – Eustace would have inherited."

"It's incredible," the Marquis exclaimed, "utterly and absolutely incredible."

Druscilla gave a little sigh.

"I told you he was dangerous," she muttered.

She felt as though her legs would hardly carry her and held onto the back of the chair for support.

"I think perhaps it would be best if you took me – home," she said weakly.

"I will," the Marquis replied. "But tell me first, Druscilla, what made you go to the coach on the other side of the square? The footman told me that there was a note for me."

"I-I – thought – " Druscilla was suddenly embarrassed. "I thought – that someone was waiting for – you there."

"Who?"

The question was like a pistol shot.

With fingers that trembled Druscilla pulled the note from where it still reposed in the breast of her dress.

Without a word she handed it to the Marquis. As he read it, she saw his lips tighten and then very slowly he tore it into small pieces.

"So you intended to interfere in my private life," he said and his voice was icy,

"I did not – want – a scandal," Druscilla stuttered. "I was – afraid – of what the Duke – might do."

"I suggest that in future," the Marquis said, throwing the pieces of the note into the wastepaper basket, "you allow me to handle my *own* affairs in my own way"

"Yes – of course," Druscilla replied meekly.

He looked at her suspiciously.

"And I mean that," he insisted. "Don't interfere, Druscilla, in what concerns me. I regret very deeply that this has happened, it must have been terrifying for you, at the same time it should be a lesson to you."

There was so much reproof in his voice that Druscilla's embarrassment and feeling of humility was swept away.

"Very well," she declared, her spirit returning, "another time I will allow them to murder you. But I hope before you encourage your cousin Eustace in his pretensions, you will at least make a will in my favour."

"Encourage Eustace!" the Marquis expostulated.

He glared across the room at Druscilla, who faced him proudly.

She was very pale and rather dishevelled and because she was so small there was something very valiant in the way that she lifted her chin and challenged the Marquis.

Quite suddenly he capitulated.

"Druscilla, you little devil! You twist yourself out of any tangle, however difficult. Very well, I will make out a will in your favour and do my best s circumvent Eustace. But another time don't open notes that are intended for me."

"I think it a pity those men did not get a chance of 'konking' you on the head," Druscilla maintained.

He laughed.

"You are a little spitfire, are you not? But God, you have courage! Most women would be having the vapours after having been through an experience such as this. Come on, Druscilla, I will take you home and I suppose that there is nothing we can say about this to anyone."

"What about Eustace?" she asked.

"What can I do? You cannot prove it was him. Are you prepared to go into the witness box and describe what happened? It would cause a most unsavoury scandal, would it not? And it would humiliate the whole family. No, I must just be on my guard, at any rate until I have made my will."

"I am sorry," Druscilla stated in a low voice, "I should not have said that."

She lowered her head feeling suddenly ashamed of her rudeness. The Marquis walked across the room to her side.

He looked down at her with a strange expression in his eyes.

"You have the courage of twenty lions," he said softly. "Under the circumstances I will forgive you anything even when you spit at me!"

She then laughed, but he could see that she was really exhausted.

"Take my arm," he suggested, "or would you like me to carry you?"

"No," she answered, "I am all right. But could I – not have – my present?"

The Marquis's eyes twinkled.

"There speaks the eternal woman!" he joked. "After all you have been through, you can still remember that you have been promised a present."

"It is many years since I have ever received a gift of any sort," Druscilla explained. "In fact since my mother died I don't remember ever having one. My father had no time for such frivolities."

"Poor Druscilla," the Marquis replied in a kind voice, "that is something we must remedy in the future. Well then, here is your first present from me. I bought it because I thought I ought to give it to you. Now I present it with real pleasure and a great deal of gratitude. Thank you, Druscilla, for saving my life."

The he took a little pink leather box from the desk and put it into her hand.

Druscilla opened it and gave a cry of sheer delight. It contained a ring, a large diamond ring encircled with other diamonds.

"It's lovely!" she exclaimed. "Is it really for me?"

"An engagement ring, but you and I know that it symbolises something else."

"What is that?" Druscilla asked, her eyes shining.

"Another adventure for the adventuress," he smiled.

There was something in his expression that made her feel strangely breathless.

CHAPTER FIVE

"Only four more days to your Wedding," the Dowager was saying to Druscilla as they walked together up the stairs to change their gowns for dinner.

"Yes, only four more days!" Druscilla repeated and knew as she reached her bedchamber that she was relieved at the thought.

Once she and the Marquis were married they would be leaving London for Lynche Hall and after that Valdo was considering whether they should go abroad to France or Italy.

Wherever they might go, Druscilla felt that some of the strain that they had been living under during these past weeks would be over.

They would be away from Eustace and free from the fears that he might strike again. She knew that his hatred was constantly in the Marquis's mind as it was in hers.

By tacit agreement and without putting it into words, they never spoke of Eustace, but the shadow of his enmity was never far from their consciousness.

Druscilla found herself looking out for him at the parties, balls and assemblies that he was inevitably invited to on account of his family and rank.

But, if he was present on any occasion, he never approached her. Sometimes when they happened to meet face to face he would make her an over-elaborate bow and she felt that there was a mocking challenge in his dark eyes as if he dared her to denounce him for what he had done or had at least attempted to do.

She knew without being told that the Marquis was careful to be constantly in the company of friends.

He did not walk home alone from St. James's Street to Berkeley Square, as he had often done in the past.

If he went riding, Sir Anthony or one of his other friends accompanied him and on the pretence that he feared there might be a robbery at his house in Berkeley Square or at the Dowager's mansion in Curzon Street, additional precautions were taken when the footmen locked the doors at night and fastened the windows.

He also replaced the old and rather decrepit nightwatchmen with younger men.

All the same the menace of Eustace was always in their thoughts and Druscilla hoped that once they could get away from London she would feel less tense and less on edge than she did at the moment.

Her thoughts inevitably dwelt at least as much on Eustace as on her marriage, but sometimes at night she would lie awake wondering what her life with the Marquis, once they were alone, would be like.

It was difficult for her to imagine it.

When she thought of Lynche Hall, she could only remember herself as a child running wild amongst the vast gardens, the shrubberies and the pine woods, which she had peopled in her imagination with dragons, witches and all sorts of mythical characters.

The Marquis had always seemed to her like a young Knight bringing excitement and adventure into her lonely existence. It was sometimes hard to remember that Valdo the boy and the Marquis the man were one and the same.

She often wondered what he was really thinking about her now that her social success was assured with the knocker on the Dowager's house rapping from dawn until dusk with invitations, callers and bouquets of flowers.

He no longer had to fear the sneers of his friends or the questions of the curious as to why he was marrying her.

But had they grown any nearer to knowing each other by being bound by the guilty secret of their marriage at The Castle or by the fear of Eustace's fatal antagonism?

The answer was 'no' because Druscilla found it almost impossible ever to be alone with the Marquis.

Since that first day when they had driven together in Hyde Park, he had not invited her to accompany him save when they were chaperoned by the Dowager or joined by Sir Anthony Headley.

There had been, it was indeed true, many other engagements to occupy their time.

They had driven down to Ranelagh, they had visited Vauxhall Gardens and there had been a ball or assembly every night of the week, but they had travelled to and from each place of entertainment in the company of other guests and never alone.

Soon they would be alone at Lynche Hall, Druscilla told herself. The thought gave her an unusual sensation that she could not explain.

Then she was sure that it was her delighted anticipation at seeing Lynche Hall again and knowing that she could live there in the great house and let its beauty, its majesty and its history, or at least in part, be hers.

She thought how often she had dreamt about it after her father had taken her away to live on the Windleham Estate and yet always in her dreams the sunshine, the beauty and the excitement had been indissolubly mixed with the boy Valdo.

She could hear his voice calling to her, commanding her to do this, directing her to do that, and she would be running to obey him, flattered and pleased that he needed her company.

Only four more days!

"Oh, the relief!" Druscilla exclaimed aloud sitting down at her dressing table. "No further fittings!"

Her wardrobes were already full of gowns, elegant, expensive and romantic such as she had never thought to own, which she had never dreamt would frame her beauty, turning her from a very ugly duckling into what she privately described to herself as a Bird of Paradise.

She had intended to be sensational from the very moment of her appearance in London and she had contrived to keep people talking and speculating about her until it seemed that overnight she had become the vogue.

She knew that she was the most fêted young woman in London, even though some of the more envious Mamas with eligible daughters looked on her coldly.

"Sometimes I think they hate me," she complained to the Dowager after she had been snubbed by one of the *Grandes Dames* of the old school.

"Of course they do," the Dowager chuckled, "it's not surprising. They have plain little *debutantes* to marry off and you have captured one of the choicest plums in the social fruitcake. They have a right to be piqued!"

"At least I have laid the suspicion that Valdo is marrying me for anything but myself," Druscilla said in a low voice.

"Undoubtedly a love match," the Dowager smiled but with a note of sarcasm in her voice.

Druscilla raised her eyes at that and asked,

"Is that what they believe? Well, I hope they continue to do so."

"That is up to you and, of course, my grandson."

"Yes, of course," Druscilla agreed. "But I am not his type, am I?"

"He had always appeared to favour fair women," the Dowager answered, making no pretence to misunderstand. There was the Duchess and a large number of pretty butterfly creatures whose names I can hardly remember. Yes, they were all fair and his mistress is the same."

"His mistress?"

Druscilla spoke harshly.

There was a sudden stillness about her, which attracted the Dowager's attention.

"I am sorry, my child, I should not have said that. I thought you knew."

"No, I did not know, but it is – of course of – no consequence."

"Of course not. Smart young men must prove their masculinity by sporting a mistress as they sport a fine piece of horseflesh."

"Who is – she?" Druscilla enquired in a low voice.

The Dowager hesitated and then replied,

"Bianca de Silva."

"The actress!" Druscilla exclaimed.

"If you can call her that," the Dowager said scathingly. "She was engaged at Covent Garden, I understand, because she displays a good deal more of her body than most young women are prepared to do."

"I did not notice her particularly – the night we went," Druscilla said, "but I remember her name. It was – on the playbills."

She wrinkled her forehead in an effort to recall Bianca de Silva's appearance.

"She is not worth your consideration," the Dowager came in tartly. "'Bits of muslin,' which is not a subject that ladies should discuss, are just pretty flowers that men pick when they are in bloom and throw away as soon as they fade. It is women like the Duchess who do far more harm and are far more dangerous than any nitwitted little doxy."

"I am sure you are right, ma'am," Druscilla agreed.

But at the same time the thought of the Marquis having a mistress perturbed her. She did not know why. She was sure that the Dowager spoke the truth when she had said that it was fashionable for a young man to have his mistress who he could show off to his friends.

Preferably one who was desired by other men to give his conquest a poignancy that might otherwise have hardly made the expense worthwhile.

What was Bianca de Silva like? If only she could remember!

She had a longing to ask that they should visit Covent Garden again, but she knew that to do so after such a conversation would make the Dowager scornful of her curiosity.

'Why should I care?' she asked herself. 'It is not of the slightest interest to me how many women he has or to whom he proffers his protection or his attention. So long as he treats me with due respect as his wife and so long as I am the Mistress of his house and his estates, it is no business of mine what he does at other times.'

She tried to tell herself to count her blessings and to remember how lucky she was.

Only a month ago she had been incarcerated in a schoolroom with no one to talk to save a small child and the servants, with extra tasks being heaped upon her and with the ever lurking fear of some gentleman taking a fancy to her despite her every effort to make herself unattractive.

"And now look at me!" Druscilla cried aloud.

She jumped up from the dressing table and moved across the room to where there was a long mirror set in the door of the wardrobe.

She stood staring at her reflection, at the glowing fires in her elegantly coiffured hair, at the whiteness of her skin and the elegance of her high-waisted dress, which revealed the exquisite lines of her slim figure without in any way overstepping the bounds of respectability.

Then her eyes went to her face and she saw reflected in the searching darkness of her eyes a question that she would not acknowledge even to herself.

'I am happy!' she declared defiantly out loud.

The words seemed to ring round the room as her maid opened the door and came in with the gown that she was to wear that evening.

The ball was to be at Devonshire House and was not only the most prestigious ball of the Season but almost the last.

After the Wedding the Prince Regent had announced his intention of leaving for Brighton and there were few people who cared to spend money on hospitality when the majority of the Prince Regent's set had left London.

"What am I wearing tonight, Rose?" Druscilla asked her maid as she watched her lay down on the bed the gown that she had carried through the passages protected by a white sheet.

"Her Ladyship thought that pale green gauze would become you best, miss," Rose answered, "and she thought tonight you would wish to wear the pearl set. The necklace is ever so beautiful."

"Yes, of course," Druscilla nodded.

But, when the pearl and diamond necklace lay open on the dressing table, she looked at it with a little shudder.

"I have always been told that pearls mean tears," she commented, half-speaking to herself.

"Oh, no, miss," Rose protested, "that's only if you wear them on your Weddin' day. At any other time they're lucky or so her Ladyship always says."

"I am sure her Ladyship knows," Druscilla said and inexpressibly felt her spirits rise.

She would have been dishonest if she had not acknowledged that she looked very lovely in the green gauze gown and she might have been a nymph emerging from the mist that rose above the lake at Lynche Hall early in the morning.

The pearls seemed almost pink against the whiteness of her skin and there was a bracelet of pearls and diamonds to clasp around one of her wrists.

But she refused the ring that went with the set, preferring her own ring of diamonds, which the Marquis had given her.

Ever since he had presented it to her that night after the frightening experience of taking his place that had saved his life, she had seldom taken the ring from her finger.

'It's my own,' she thought a thousand times, 'my very own piece of jewellery.'

She had worn it even to go to bed. Sometimes there seemed to be a sparkle of fire in the stones, which was echoed by a sudden sparkle within herself.

It was like an excitement that she had never known before and a thrill such as she had never believed possible and yet in some strange way it was anticipation more than reality.

"You look really lovely, miss," Rose remarked sincerely as she made ready to leave the bedroom. "I am real sure his Lordship will think so."

"I hope so," Druscilla smiled. "Thank you, Rose."

But, when she had gone downstairs to join the dinner party, it seemed to her that the Marquis was more preoccupied than usual and that his greeting was conventionally polite but nothing more.

They drove to Devonshire House. The Dowager was with them together with an old beau of hers, now a retired General, who insisted on lecturing them on the inadequacy of British preparations against Napoleon should he recommence hostilities.

He talked pompously and Druscilla found her attention wandering.

She glanced across the carriage at the Marquis.

It was not yet completely dark outside, although the sun had sunk in a burst of crimson glory and the first stars were just beginning to twinkle in the sky.

By the light from the carriage window she could see that he looked tired and she wondered if indeed Eustace's threats were worrying him more than he would ever admit.

Then she remembered that after they had left the dinner party the night before, the Marquis had seemed particularly lively and high-spirited when they said 'goodnight'.

She had had a suspicion that he was going on to another party and now she was sure of it. He had been up late, very late, that was obvious, but who had he spent the time with?

It was the question that she could not help asking herself.

Their horses carried them through the magnificently ornamented gold-tipped gates of Devonshire House.

There was the usual crush of coaches and carriages, of linkmen with flaring torches, footmen in gold braid helping to assist the bejewelled guests onto the red carpet that led into the vast hall with its curving staircase, marble statues and huge more than life-size portraits of the fascinating Devonshires.

"One thing we can be sure of here," the Marquis said as they waited on the stairs to be received, "is that we shall have a good game of cards."

"Then I shall join you for a short while," the Dowager announced. "I am tired of sitting on uncomfortable chairs in noisy ballrooms. Not that I intend to play for high stakes. I cannot afford your extravagance when it comes to gambling."

"Nonsense, Grandmama," the Marquis replied. "You are as warm-fingered as any of us when it comes to a wager. Besides, if my memory is not at fault, you always win."

The Dowager chuckled.

"Not always," she corrected, "but when I was young and lost it did not unduly perturb me. I have always believed in the saying, *unlucky at cards, lucky in love.*"

"You cannot say that to Valdo, ma'am," Sir Anthony intervened. "If he wins tonight, he will be apprehensive as to what Miss Morley is doing. And if nothing else that should fetch him from the card room."

"Don't listen to him," Druscilla smiled at the Marquis. "I know how much you dislike dancing. If I am short of partners, I will come and find you."

The Marquis glanced at her gratefully.

"I must say, Druscilla, that you are a good deal more considerate than some females."

They shook hands with the Duke and Duchess of Devonshire and Druscilla was immediately besieged by a number of young bucks demanding that she dance with them.

By the time she had promised away more than a dozen dances, she looked round to see that both the Marquis and the Dowager had disappeared.

"I am unchaperoned," she said to Sir Anthony, who had claimed the first dance. "Do you imagine the Powers-that-be on the dais will condemn me for it?"

Sir Anthony glanced towards the tiaraed Dowagers who sat on a raised platform, many of them with lorgnettes, inspecting the dancers with critical eyes.

"They are like a lot of old hens clucking away," he said, "and you can be certain that they are not saying anything nice about anyone, not even about themselves!"

"Perhaps one day I shall be sitting amongst them," Druscilla smiled. "It's a sobering thought, is it not?"

"You have too much spirit and are far too beautiful ever to look like them, however old you may grow," he replied.

She smiled at him and then saw something in his eyes that made her drop her own.

"Druscilla – " Sir Anthony began in a low voice.

She lifted her hand and put her fingers against his lips.

"No, don't say – it."

"How do you know what I am going to say?" he asked.

"I can guess," Druscilla replied, "and it will spoil everything. I have been so happy in having your friendship and at the moment I am in need of – friends."

"It's not friendship I feel for you," Sir Anthony said. "Damn Valdo, why did I not meet you first?"

"Please let's go on being friends," Druscilla insisted. "I cannot explain, but both Valdo and I rely on you. You are of great import to us both."

The expression that she had feared in Sir Anthony's eyes faded a little.

"I want only to be of service to you, Druscilla and, of course, to – Valdo. It's just that sometimes a man cannot help his feelings."

"But he need not express them. Please, Anthony, promise me that you will keep whatever you are feeling to yourself."

She had used his Christian name without realising it, as he led her from the dance floor onto the balcony overlooking the garden.

"You are so lovely, Druscilla," he said hoarsely, "you drive a man mad, you make him forget everything else in life, his loyalty, his code of honour, everything except a love that he cannot control."

"I don't think you really love me," she demurred.

Sir Anthony would have protested, but she held up her hand.

"No, let me finish. You are interested in me, perhaps I excite you a little because I am a new face and a new person. But that is not love, not love as it should be, not love as I think it is."

"Then what is love?" Sir Anthony asked in a deep voice.

Druscilla thought for several seconds while he watched her.

"I think," she said at length, "real love is simply being a part of another person and he of you. Whatever they may be like, attractive or unattractive, bad or good, it does not matter, it is just something which cannot be explained."

There was silence for a moment.

Then she shook her head.

"Don't listen to me, I am talking nonsense. I have never been in love, but that is what I think – it should be like."

"And that is how I could love you if you loved me," Sir Anthony declared. "It's not too late, Druscilla. Run away with me, tonight, tomorrow, any moment before next Tuesday when you will be married to Valdo."

"And what would Valdo do?" Druscilla asked him.

"He would survive somehow," Sir Anthony said impatiently and she was aware that, without putting it into words, he knew that the Marquis was not in love with her.

"Thank you, Anthony dear, for asking me," she said gently. "If it was possible I might even have considered it a long time ago, but now it is too late."

"Too late?" he questioned.

Druscilla nodded her head.

"Much too late," she answered firmly..

"Miss Morley, I have been looking for you everywhere, this is our dance," a voice came from behind them.

She turned from Sir Anthony, knowing that their conversation was at an end, but a little saddened by the stricken expression on his face.

'He will get over it' she thought and concentrated during the next two hours on living up to her reputation for sparkling repartee.

It was nearly one o'clock in the morning when she realised that she felt rather tired and had not yet been down to supper. It was too hot to stay indoors and the thought of eating had no attraction for her.

In the garden behind Devonshire House the trees and flowerbeds were illuminated by tiny flickering lights making the whole place a Fairyland of beauty.

There were fountains throwing their sparkling water high against the starlit sky and there were tiny arbours covered in roses and honeysuckle with soft cushioned seats for those who were brave enough to defy the conventions.

Druscilla wandered down the path beside her last partner, a rather pompous young man in the Life Guards. He was beginning to bore her with a long story of how badly his horses had run at Ascot the previous week.

His voice droned on and Druscilla suddenly decided that she had had enough of him.

"I am thirsty," she said plaintively, "I wander if you would be kind enough to bring me a drink."

"It would be a pleasure," he said gallantly. "What would you prefer, champagne?"

Druscilla shook her head.

"No, indeed, I think it would make me thirstier. Perhaps a glass of lemonade."

"I will procure one for you immediately, Miss Morley," he offered.

He looked round and saw a small unoccupied arbour to the left of them.

"Will you wait here for me? I will be as swift as I can."

"Thank you, you are very kind."

Druscilla sat herself on the arbour, glad to be free for the moment of so much conversation.

A yew hedge with topiary work divided the garden on one side of the arbour and was, she felt, some protection from the curious eyes of gentlemen walking alone who might have taken it into their heads to join her.

She leant back against the cushions and closed her eyes.

Then, as she was almost dozing, she realised that someone was standing in the opening of the arbour.

"How quick you have been – " she began and then gave a little cry of sheer terror.

*

In the card room the Dowager gathered together her winnings and rose from the table.

"It's after midnight and I must retire to bed," she remarked. "I wonder where Druscilla can be found."

The Marquis, who had been seated at the same table, also rose.

"Shall I look for her, ma'am?"

The Dowager shook her head.

"Let the child enjoy herself, but tell her I have gone home. When she is ready to leave, you can escort her. I will send back the carriage."

"Very well, Grandmama," the Marquis said. "I believe the real reason you are leaving is that you are in a hurry to get home with your ill-gotten gains. Thanks to you my pockets are to let."

"And mine!" one of the other players at the table agreed ruefully.

"You flatter me," the Dowager said delightedly. "You know as well as I do that if I had not been such a restraining influence you would have plunged far deeper."

"I can only say that with your luck, ma'am, I am thankful you are not a member of White's Club," one of the gentlemen declared as he kissed her gloved hand.

The Marquis escorted the Dowager downstairs and saw her into her coach.

"Don't let Druscilla be too late," she admonished him as the footman closed the door.

The Marquis walked back upstairs towards the ballroom. There was no sign of Druscilla and he sauntered down to the supper room, talking with various acquaintances on the way. But, although he glanced at every table, he could not see his future wife.

"Where is Druscilla?" he asked Sir Anthony, meeting him on the stairway.

"I have not seen her for some time," Sir Anthony replied. "It's stiflingly hot, if you ask me, she will be in the garden."

"I expect that is where I shall find her," the Marquis said languidly and left Sir Anthony to take his partner up to the airless ballroom.

The Marquis walked slowly down the garden.

He noticed the arbours and recognised that it would be embarrassing to peer closely into them. At the same time there was no sign of Druscilla on the paths that wound their way between the fountains and the fragrant flowerbeds.

As he moved across the grass, he suddenly heard Druscilla's voice.

"Leave me alone! Don't you dare come near me!"

Her tone was sharp, but there was no mistaking an undercurrent of fear.

"Do you really think I would let you escape me?" a man's voice answered. "I have been looking for you, thinking of you and aching for you. I could not believe when I returned to London that it was you who everyone was talking about."

"I am engaged to be married," Druscilla asserted defiantly. "If you insult me, my fiancé will deal with you."

"Do you think I am frightened by a young whippersnapper like that?" the man enquired. "And whether you are engaged or married, Druscilla, it matters not where you and I are concerned."

"Let me pass – I will not stay here and listen to you," Druscilla cried.

"You will not get away as easily as that," was the reply. "I want you, Druscilla, *my God*, how I want you! It drives me mad even to think about you. That white skin of yours. Do you imagine that a man can once touch you and not long to do so again? Damme, but you were lovely in the firelight, do you think I could ever forget?"

"Let me – go!"

The Marquis heard Druscilla almost scream the words and then there was silence as though someone had placed a hand over her mouth.

He had stood listening almost stupidly, but now suddenly he was galvanised into action.

But where was she? Her voice had come from the other side of the yew hedge.

He put out his hands to try to separate the trees, but realised that they were wired together and there was no way through them.

He started to run towards the end of the hedge that stretched halfway across the garden and then, as he rounded it, he met Druscilla rushing towards him, her dress streaming out behind her, her arms outstretched and her head thrown back.

She was running so swiftly that she collided with him before she realised who it was.

"Oh – Valdo! *Valdo!*"

He heard the relief in her voice and felt her hands clutching at him.

"Take me – away – take me – away!"

"Who is that man, what has he done to you?" the Marquis demanded.

He stared over her shoulder and into the darkness. It was impossible to see anyone in the shadows of the yew hedge.

"Only take me – away," Druscilla cried, "I cannot stay – here, I cannot – "

The Marquis put his arm round her and realised that she was trembling and that her breath was coming brokenly from her lips.

She was frightened almost to madness as he had seen men terrified the first time that they came under enemy fire.

"It's all right," he told her soothingly. "No one shall hurt you. But who the hell was it?"

"Take me – away, only – take me away," Druscilla moaned.

The Marquis looked down at her. Seeing the terror in her face he led her not towards the house but away from it down the garden, while she fought for breath like a man who had been running in a Marathon race.

"It's all right," he kept comforting her.

They stopped nearly at the bottom of the garden and Druscilla suddenly clutched at the Marquis's arm.

"I will – not go – back. I will not see – him again! I – cannot. You don't – understand."

"We need not go back to the house," the Marquis said. "There is a way out here, I will take you home."

There was a door in the high wall that led into Berkeley Street. There was a footman in attendance on it, who opened it for the Marquis and closed it behind them.

In the street outside was a long row of coaches and carriages waiting until they should be called to the entrance in Piccadilly to take their owners home.

The Marquis walked up to the carriage that stood opposite the door that they had just emerged from.

"I am the Marquis of Lynche," he addressed the coachman. "This lady is ill and I wish to take her back to Curzon Street. It is only a short distance and I know that your Master," he turned and looked at the Coat of Arms on the panel, "Lord Belton, would not object to your obliging us."

"Very good, my Lord," the coachman replied.

The footman jumped down to open the door and take the nosebags off the horses. Then the coach turned and started to carry them the short way to Curzon Street.

Druscilla sat huddled in the corner of the coach, her hands up to her face. She did not speak and nor did the Marquis until the coach set them down outside the Dowager's house.

The night-footman let them in and the Marquis, having thrown a guinea to the coachman, walked into the house after her.

"Has her Ladyship retired?" he asked the footman.

"Some time ago, my Lord."

"Then light the tapers in the small salon and the fire as well," the Marquis commanded.

The footman looked surprised, but hurriedly did as he was told.

The Marquis, taking Druscilla by the arm, led her into the salon on the ground floor, which was usually used by the Dowager in the mornings.

There was the fragrance of flowers and the perfume of pot-pourri. The footman kindled the fire and the Marquis filled a glass from the table near the door and brought it to Druscilla.

"I don't – want – anything," she muttered shaking her head.

"Drink it," the Marquis ordered.

She did as she was told because there was no point in arguing.

Only when she took the first sip did she realise that he had given her brandy and the fiery spirit seemed to sear its way down her throat and stop the trembling that was shaking her whole body.

The footman left the room and she moved from the sofa onto the soft fur rug in front of the fire. The flames were just beginning to lick the kindling sticks and she held out her hands towards them.

The Marquis sat down in a chair watching her.

"It was Walden, was it not?"

She nodded her head.

"I think you will have to tell me what happened," the Marquis suggested.

She looked at him and instinctively a denial rose to her lips.

"No – no – I could – not."

"I have a right to know," the Marquis insisted quietly. "I heard what he said to you, I must know what he meant by saying that he had touched you. You can understand that."

Druscilla drew a deep breath and dropped her hands into her lap and her head fell forward. For a moment she looked very young and very defenceless, little more than a child who had been punished unjustly.

But the Marquis's eyes were hard as he persisted abruptly.

"I have to know, Druscilla.

There was a long silence and he thought that once again she was going to refuse.

Then suddenly she began to speak.

Her voice was broken and breathless, she stumbled over her words, speaking in such a low tone that at times he could hardly hear her and yet she talked on and on almost as if it was a relief to be able to confide in him.

She told him how she had been engaged by Lady Walden as Governess to their children, arriving with an already smeared reputation and already humiliated by what she had suffered in previous employment.

She spoke frankly and without exaggeration of the insults she had received and it was easy for the man listening to fill in so much that she left unsaid and to understand so much that she did not explain.

At first Druscilla felt that in Lord Walden's house she had found a refuge from all she had suffered before.

Lady Walden was dull and rather stiff, but pleasant enough when the occasion demanded and she seemed to approve of the way that her new Governess was teaching the children.

After a time, Druscilla, at first tense and fearful, began to relax and to feel that she need no longer be on the defensive and no longer afraid.

Lord Walden was away. He was, she learnt, at their house in London, while Lady Walden, who was delicate, found the winter easier to endure in the country where there were not so many social engagements.

When Lord Walden had first returned to his house, Druscilla was not alarmed.

A man nearing middle age, he did not appear to her of any particular presence until one evening, as she fetched the children from the drawing room to take them to bed, he brushed against her as she was passing the door.

It was only a touch on her bare arm, but it was enough! Every instinct in her body signalled danger.

The following day he had come to the schoolroom shortly after lunch. She had risen to her feet as he entered, quickly slipping her disguising spectacles onto her nose.

She knew that it was the time when Lady Walden lay down to rest. The children were also resting, although she was thankful that the door into the night nursery was open and there was no reason for him to suppose that they were asleep.

"Good afternoon, Miss Morley," Lord Walden had said.

She had dropped him a small curtsey.

"Good afternoon, my Lord."

"Sit down," he had said. "I have only called to see if you are comfortable, if you have everything you want."

"Everything, thank you, my Lord."

"And the children are good and obedient? You like being here?"

"Very much, my Lord."

"That is good, very good."

Druscilla had been sitting near the fire and now he stood in front of it. A big man and broad-shouldered he thrust his hands into the pockets of his coat and stood looking down at her.

"Are you not rather young, Miss Morley, for this employment?"

"Well, my Lord, I have been teaching for over two years."

"You have red hair, Miss Morley. It somehow belies the subservient tone you use to me."

"I am sorry if – my voice does not – please your Lordship."

"Your hair *does* please me," he commented ominously. "But a little more spirit, a little more fire perhaps, might be expected in a woman whose hair is the colour of yours."

"They are surely not attributes one would expect from a Governess to your children, my Lord."

She glanced up at him as she spoke, meaning to reprove him both by her expression and by her words.

Instead she saw in his eyes the look that she had grown to fear and a sudden terror made her heart pound and her voice die away in her throat.

For a moment he stared down at her and then abruptly, as though he controlled himself with an effort, he turned and left the room.

She had known then that the peace she had found was over, her sense of security was finished and she was afraid – afraid as she had never been afraid before.

Days passed without any particular incident taking place, save that she had known by the way Lord Walden looked at her when they met, by the excuses he invented to send for his children so that she could accompany them, that it was only a question of time before he approached her.

She wondered frantically what she could do about it. She could not leave, there was nowhere she could go.

To give in her notice would mean that she would have to return once again to the Domestic Bureau where they had already told her that they were unlikely to find her any more positions without references and with such a short stay in each prior engagement.

Then one dark night at the end of March, she was just returning to bed when a message came that Lady Walden wished to speak to her.

"At ten o'clock – at night?" she queried.

The housemaid who had carried the message said,

"I was just helpin' tidy her Ladyship's room with her maid when she says to me, 'tell Miss Morley I wish to speak to her'."

"Was his Lordship – there?" Druscilla asked.

"Not in the room," the housemaid replied, "but he was next door. I sees him."

Druscilla hesitated. Dare she send a reply to say that she had retired for the night? She somehow knew that it would be useless,

She looked round the schoolroom.

With the fire burning in the hearth and the candles lit, it looked warm and cosy, a sanctuary of refuge. Yet she must leave it, the housemaid was waiting.

"Very well," Druscilla said, "I will – come."

She closed the door behind her and walked down the passage.

She tried to think why Lady Walden should have sent for her, but she could remember nothing that the children had done wrong or she herself had omitted.

The schoolroom was some way from the main part of the house. By the time she reached it Druscilla felt cold from the chill in the passages and cold from her nervous anticipation of what was wrong.

She knocked at the bedroom door.

"Come in."

Lady Walden was in bed, propped up against her pillows. She looked ill.

Her health was undermined every year, Druscilla had learnt, by the bronchial attacks that kept her almost permanently in bed during the winter months.

Druscilla entered quietly.

She glanced round the room and saw with a sense of deep relief that Lord Walden was not present.

"Come in, Miss Morley," Lady Walden had said in a faint voice, "I wish to speak with you."

"Is anything wrong, my Lady? I do hope you are feeling better."

"A little better, thank you," Lady Walden replied.

"Is it about the children?"

"His Lordship has a suspicion that they have been playing in the kitchen garden again."

"But it is not true, my Lady," Druscilla had retorted. "The children have not been near the kitchen garden since you spoke about it before."

"His Lordship asked me to speak to you, Miss Morley. You know how difficult it is to find good gardeners these days and Bennett has been with us for years. If he is upset, his Lordship is afraid he might retire and we would never be able to replace him with anyone so good."

"Yes, I quite understand, your Ladyship, but I promise you the children have not been in the kitchen garden or at any time in the greenhouses. I have been with them all the time."

"Then that is excellent," Lady Walden said. "I was sure that his Lordship was mistaken, but he was insistent that I should speak to you at once in case anything happened tomorrow."

"But why tomorrow?" Druscilla enquired.

"I don't know," Lady Walden replied, "it is just his Lordship's idea that Bennett might want to see him to complain."

"I promise you that will not happen," Druscilla said soothingly. "So please don't worry yourself. I shall be with the children every minute, your Ladyship, and – they will not go anywhere without me."

"I trust you. Miss Morley," Lady Walden smiled, "and I am very pleased with the way Lucy is getting on with her lessons."

"Thank you," Druscilla said and curtseyed. "Good night, my Lady."

"Good night, Miss Morley."

Druscilla had sped back down the passages with a light heart.

So it had not been anything so frightening after all, only Lord Walden fussing about the gardener, who was a crusty old man and ready to find fault on every possible occasion.

Though why his Lordship should have put the idea into his head that the children had been in the kitchen garden she could not think.

She reached the schoolroom a little breathless from the rate that she had hurried along the passages at.

She opened the door and felt momentarily perplexed.

The candles were out and the room was in darkness save for the light of the fire, which cast a warm glow over the fur rug.

Then she screamed and her heart leapt suffocatingly into her throat because he came from behind the door and caught her arms.

CHAPTER SIX

Druscilla's voice died into silence and the Marquis could see all too clearly that she was reliving that moment of terror.

The flames were leaping higher in the fireplace and the light from them glinted on her red hair, turning it into an enchantment of living gold.

But her eyes were dark with fear and her lips trembled, while her slender fingers entwined themselves one with another. Leaning back in the armchair and watching her, the Marquis did not speak.

After a moment Druscilla continued,

"They say that when a man drowns his whole life flashes before his eyes. In that instant I saw all too clearly how Lord Walden – had plotted so that he would have access to – the schoolroom, which I always kept locked after the children went to bed – "

She had fought against him, fought and struggled, but all the time she had been aware of his great strength. His arms seemed to encompass her like bands of steel, while his face, drawing nearer and nearer to hers in the darkness, was all the more frightening because she could not see him clearly.

Holding her with one arm he turned to lock the door and in that moment she escaped from his grasp.

She ran across the room, trying to put the table between herself and him, but he caught her easily.

As he did so, he gave a laugh of triumph and she knew that the only thing she had done was to inflame his desires and that her endeavours to elude him merely added to his sense of excitement.

Slowly and relentlessly while she struggled and twisted and turned in his arms, he drew her towards the hearth.

There, in the light of the fire, she could now see his face and knew it to be the face of the Devil. She fought him desperately knowing that, even if she had had the breath to do so, it was no use screaming.

The schoolroom wing was isolated from the rest of the house and nobody would hear her save the children themselves.

She struck at him with all her strength and tried to scratch his face. Then, even as she realised that her efforts were utterly useless, her feet slipped.

She fell down on the soft fur rug and knew in that moment that she was lost. He threw himself on top of her and started to tear her dress away from her neck.

At last she would have screamed, but her breath seemed to be strangled in her throat and she could only moan.

"Please – please – spare me," she managed to gasp.

But she knew as she spoke that, lost to all decency, he did not even hear her.

The cheap cotton of her gown gave beneath his destructive fingers. She heard it tear and knew that the firelight was now on her naked breasts.

'Save me – oh, God – *save me*!" she cried out, her voice ringing out unexpectedly clear and she prayed and prayed.

She felt his hands, they were those of a man demented, a man driven by passion until he was hardly human – primitive and uncivilised and little more than a beast.

And then, when she felt that she must die, when she knew that nothing could save her but a miracle, half-unconscious with terror and at the same time nauseated and revolted by the proximity of the monster who would possess her, her prayer was answered.

She was gasping for breath, conscious that any further resistance was useless as he tore at her skirt, when a small voice came from the doorway,

"I'm thirsty, can I have a glass of water, please?"

Lord Walden was suddenly still.

Raising himself, he turned his head almost automatically towards the darkness that the sound of his child's voice had come from.

In that moment Druscilla was free.

Somehow she scrambled to her feet and, clutching the tattered remnants of what had once been her gown she ran, her breath coming raspingly between her lips, towards the child who stood in the half-open door of the night nursery.

She put her arms round the little girl and pushed her back into the bedroom.

She slammed the door, locked it and in spite of the child's frightened cry, started to pile the furniture in front of it.

She moved the chest of drawers, the chairs and even the wardrobe – furniture the weight of which ordinarily she would have found far beyond her strength, but now in her desperation became somehow movable.

She piled the pieces up in her frenzy, while the children, by the light of the flickering night light, watched her at first in silence until they broke into frightened tears.

"Why are you doing that, Miss Morley?"

"Why are you frightened?"

"Who has torn your gown?"

It was the six-year-old Lucy who was the more perceptive, while the younger child who had asked for the water merely cried because something was happening that she did not understand.

Only when practically every piece of furniture in the bedroom was piled in front of the door did Druscilla collapse onto the floor to lie there semi-conscious in the cold and darkness.

Finally the children, both pulling at her with terrified hands, made her remember her responsibility towards them.

Wearily, moving like a very old woman, she dragged herself to her feet, put on her dressing gown and persuaded them to go back to bed.

"It's – all right," she kept saying automatically, "it's – quite all right now."

But she knew for her that it would never be all right.

Never again could she enter the schoolroom without being afraid of what would come out of the shadows.

Never again could she see the hearth rug without feeling the nauseating touch of a man's hands, seeing his face contorted with lust and passion, his eyes blazing and his lips wet with desire.

Finally the children fell asleep, but she lay on top of her bed, too exhausted and too frightened even to undress.

Only when morning came did she realise the terrible predicament she was now in.

Her first impulse was to pack her baggage and leave, but she knew only too well that if she did so there would be no other employment waiting for her at the Domestic Bureau.

They had made it clear the last time that they would make no effort to accommodate her again. And so weakly, instead of leaving the house as she knew she ought to do, she sought out Lady Walden.

Crimson with embarrassment at what she had to say, incoherent, but at the same time driven by desperation, she said,

"I must ask you, my Lady, to request that Lord Walden – not to come to the schoolroom. It is difficult for me to say this, as I am sure – you will appreciate, but last night, after I returned from visiting you in your bedroom, he assaulted me."

She would have said more but Lady Walden interrupted.

"I have already heard his Lordship's version of your behaviour, Miss Morley," she said in an icy voice. "You will leave this house immediately. I will give you no reference and, as I do not consider you a fit person to be in charge of my children, you will forfeit the wages that are owing to you."

"But that is not fair!" Druscilla cried hotly. "I shall have been here a month tomorrow – you cannot turn me out without a penny."

Lady Walden turned her face away.

"His Lordship has already told me how tiresome you have been importuning him and making yourself a general nuisance as far as he is concerned. I feel we have no obligation towards you, Miss Morley."

"His Lordship said – that!" Druscilla almost screamed.

"I do *not* think, Miss Morley," Lady Walden continued, "that either your appearance or talents are what are required in the schoolroom of a gentleman's house. I suggest that you find employment where you will not be in the company of either ladies such as myself or of their children."

For the moment Druscilla was too stunned to reply.

Then before she could speak Lady Walden said,

"That will be all, Miss Morley. This interview is now terminated."

Druscilla had gone from the room feeling more outraged than humiliated.

Then, as she walked down the passage, her eyes bright with anger and seething with an almost uncontrollable rage, she realised that she was completely and utterly penniless.

She went into the bedroom to find that the children had gone, having obviously been taken for a walk by one of the housemaids.

Her cheap round-topped trunk had been placed in the centre of the room. But on the table there was something else – a letter.

Even as Druscilla opened it, she knew what she would find.

There were only a few words in strong handwriting on the thick crested paper.

"*Go to 27 Lavender Lane, Regents Park.*"

Inside the envelope was a sovereign. She saw then the reason why Lord Walden had already complained about her.

He was aware what her position had been when she came to the house, how she had been forced to admit that she had no references and that she had either been dismissed or had left her previous places of employment.

She had been deeply grateful that Lady Walden had accepted her as the children's Governess.

'He is determined to get me,' she had told herself.

If he had failed last night, the fact that he had so nearly succeeded in ravishing her merely made him all the keener.

For one moment she had thought that she would take the note and the sovereign to Lady Walden, but even as the idea crossed her mind she recognised that it would get her no further.

She would still be dismissed and still be thrown penniless onto the streets.

She looked at her face in the mirror and cursed her own beauty.

Even with her hair dragged back into a hard bun at the nape of her neck, even wearing the ugly steel-rimmed spectacles and even in the drab brown cotton dress, she could see that there was something about her appearance that could attract men, especially men like Lord Walden.

'Oh God! What am – I to do?'

Covering her face with her hands, she remembered that her prayers had saved her last night at the eleventh hour when she had felt that she was past help,

God had not failed her then, would He do so now?

She tore up the note into a dozen pieces, hating even to handle the paper because Lord Walden's fingers had touched it first, and flung it into the fire.

At first she thought of keeping the sovereign, as that at least would help her to escape.

Then she knew she could not – it was tainted because he had owned it – and going to the window she opened the casement and flung the coin as far as she could into the garden.

'Someone will find it one day,' she thought, 'and believe that they have stumbled onto treasure trove.'

Then she opened her purse. In it there was only a shilling and a few pennies, which was all she possessed in the world.

She finished packing her trunk and then went downstairs to the housekeeper's room.

A strait-laced elderly spinster, the housekeeper had been in the service of Lord Walden's father and mother.

Druscilla had known her as a martinet in the house, a woman who looked with disapproval on the young and yet was wholly just.

"I am leaving, Miss Lacey," she informed her.

"So I understand from her Ladyship," the housekeeper replied.

"I don't know what she – has told you," Druscilla went on, "but what she believes is untrue. You know that ever since I have been here I kept the door of the schoolroom locked from the moment – I put the children to bed. I have only opened it to allow my supper to be brought in and collected again. Last night someone entered while I was not – in the room."

For a moment the housekeeper did not speak.

Then, as her eyes rested on Druscilla, there was just a faint expression of sympathy.

"What can I do for you?" she asked.

"Will you lend me enough money – to get to Windleham?" Druscilla asked. "It is where my father was Vicar before he died. I am going to The Castle to ask the Duchess if she will give me some employment, if not looking after the children, perhaps working – as a sewing maid. Anything so long as I don't starve. I swear that I will pay you back. It will be a loan and I can give you no security other than – my word of honour."

The housekeeper rose to her feet.

"I will help you, Miss Morley. Life is not easy for young ladies in your position."

"Easy!" Druscilla's voice almost broke on a sob.

Then pride and her hatred for the man who had driven her to this made her raise her chin proudly.

"While there are men in the world," she said bitterly, "it will never be easy for women until – they are old and ugly and ready for the grave."

The housekeeper took some money from a well worn black purse.

"Give it me back when you can," she said, "there is no hurry. Many years ago I too suffered as you are doin' now."

"You did!" Druscilla exclaimed almost incredulously. "And what – happened?"

The housekeeper smiled a little wryly.

"In my case I thought my heart was broken, but hearts don't break very easily. I went on workin'. Now I have come to a quiet haven in my declinin' years."

"You loved the man?" Druscilla asked, wondering if the person in question had been one of Lord Walden's ancestors.

"I loved him," the housekeeper admitted with a little sigh, "but love is too often a weapon that a woman has no defence against."

"That is true," Druscilla had agreed, "and I can promise you that I will – never love a man, never, never!"

She went from the housekeeper's room with a new confidence and feeling somehow comforted that she was not alone in what she suffered and that there were other women who could understand.

Then, as the brake that was used by the staff was carrying her down the drive, she saw that Lord Walden was watching her go.

Astride one of his horses, he was deliberately waiting, she guessed, to watch her departure.

He was expecting perhaps to receive a nod of her head or a flutter of her hand to show that she had received his note and had acquiesced in his suggestion.

She made no movement of any sort as the brake passed him and he sat there staring after her. He was under the shadow of the trees and the driver may not even have seen him.

But he was only a few feet away from Druscilla and she felt that some of the evil he exuded reached out towards her to drag her once again into his eager arms.

She knew then that he would pursue her relentlessly wherever she might go and wherever she might hide.

She turned her face away, but not before she had seen a smile on his lips that told her that he remembered and gloated over her helplessness last night.

He had made her tremble and cringe and she had been powerless against his brute strength.

The brake with its two horses was drawing away from him and yet Druscilla felt the distance was not widening between them.

It seemed to her then that she could never be free of him. Every night his face would be there before her, taunting her and terrifying her.

She could never go to bed without looking to see if he was there at the door, lurking in the shadows, ready even to encroach upon her dreams.

Often she would wake up screaming in the night and know that she had dreamt once again that she was lying powerless beneath him.

It was only when she came to London after the hurried secret marriage with the Marquis that she for a time forgot Lord Walden.

There were so many other things to think about and she was so happy with the Dowager Marchioness. But now the overwhelming terror and panic that he had induced in her had returned.

As she finished her story, her voice was trembling and stumbling over her words.

She turned towards the Marquis and kneeling beside him held out her clasped hands.

"He will – seek me out," she stammered. "Now that he – knows where I am – he will – never leave me – alone. I cannot escape – from him – oh, save me – *save me*! I will die rather than let him – touch me again. Oh, God – what shall I do?"

There was sheer unrestrained terror in her voice and in her eyes. In that moment she hardly realised who she was speaking to.

The Marquis could see that she was almost hysterical.

He reached out his hands and held hers.

"Listen, Druscilla," he said and, as he realised that she had not heard him, he repeated, "Listen to me. You are safe, do you understand, completely safe. Walden will never touch you again, I swear it!"

"But he said – he would never – let me go," Druscilla gasped.

"Look at me, Druscilla," the Marquis insisted, tightening his clasp on her hands.

She looked up at him, her face very white and her eyes dark with misery and fear. It was the face of a woman, he thought, driven almost insane with terror and he said very gently in a voice which no one had ever heard from him before,

"He will not hurt you, Druscilla. I swear it and you can believe me. He will not come near you and he will not frighten you again."

"How can – you be – sure?" she stammered.

"I will make certain that he does not do so," the Marquis answered.

For a moment her face seemed to lighten and then her fingers tightened on his.

~116~

"You would fight him? No, you must not do that. It will only make – a scandal."

"I will not fight him, but I will prevent him from pestering you, that I can promise."

"But how – how?" Druscilla demanded.

"Can you not trust me?"

She looked desperately into his face as if for reassurance.

Something she saw there must have given her the courage she needed for he felt her relax.

"Do you really – promise?" she asked in a low voice, almost like a child who was afraid of the dark,

"I promise. You can go to bed, Druscilla, knowing that you will be free of all these fears that have tortured you for so long."

"But what are you going to do?" she asked. "How can you keep him away from me?"

"I will contrive it," the Marquis said with such assurance in his voice that she could not help believing him.

She tried to free her hands and he instantly released them.

"I believe you," she murmured slowly, "although what you can do – I cannot conceive."

"Don't think about him," the Marquis suggested.

Druscilla moved away from his knees back to her position in front of the fire.

"If only I could be sure – he was not – lurking somewhere – looking for me – waiting for me," she whispered almost beneath her breath.

"He will not be in future," the Marquis replied reassuringly.

She flashed him a little glance and he saw that the colour had come back into her cheeks.

"What a hopeless pair – we are," she said in an unsteady voice, making, he knew, a tremendous effort to be normal. "You have – Eustace to cope with and I have – "

"Don't say his name," the Marquis interrupted. "As far as you are concerned, he is finished, forgotten and out of your life. I have a plan. I will tell you about it tomorrow, but now you must go to bed."

Almost reluctantly it seemed Druscilla rose to her feet.

"You will not do anything – stupid?" she asked, hesitating over the words. "Besides, if you fight him, he – he might kill you and think how pleased Eustace would be then."

. "I am not yet ready to die," the Marquis smiled, "even though today I did make a will leaving you everything that is not entailed."

"I did not wish you to do that," Druscilla said sharply. "When I spoke the other night – I was in a temper, I did not mean what I said."

"All the same it was a sensible suggestion," the Marquis assured her. "I am determined that, if I must die, Eustace shall not inherit everything I possess."

"It is all horrible and – menacing," Druscilla groaned, "and I was – so happy."

"You can go on being happy," the Marquis replied. "We are not yet defeated and why should we be? So far we have won every battle, have we not, you and I?"

She looked up at him, her face transformed with a smile.

"Yes, we have won so far," she agreed. "I must not be a fool and let my apprehensions bring us – bad luck. I have been saved from so many disasters in my life, I should be grateful and sure that Fate is on my side."

"Fate is on our side," the Marquis insisted firmly, "believe that, little Druscilla. And remember that confidence is something that is of inestimable value to anyone who is doing battle. Just believe that we shall defeat my bogeyman and yours and they will both vanish into thin air."

"If only I could be sure – of that," Druscilla said.

"You can."

He took her hand and raised it to his lips,

"Go to bed, you are tired out with all you have been through. And remember you are under my protection now. No one will hurt you, no one."

She looked up into his eyes and was suddenly very still.

Something passed between them, something indefinable that brought Druscilla a strange feeling as though she could not breathe.

There was a sudden flicker within her body, almost as though a small flame awoke within herself and then the clock chimed on the mantelshelf and the spell was broken.

"It's getting late," the Marquis remarked. "Goodnight, Druscilla and sleep well."

He opened the door into the hall. At the far end a sleepy footman sitting in a big padded armchair by the front door struggled to his feet.

The Marquis and Druscilla walked together to the foot of the staircase.

"Goodnight," Druscilla murmured gently, "and thank you."

The Marquis kissed her hand and left the house while Druscilla went upstairs to her bedroom realising as she did so that she was indeed very tired.

It seemed as if the Marquis had in some way exorcised her terrors, but they were still there lurking beneath the surface.

She knew that had she gone to bed without talking with him downstairs, she would have been too distraught to sleep and too frightened even to undress and climb into bed.

She remembered how it had been impossible for her to sleep when she had first left the Walden's home and gone to The Castle.

Every night in the darkness she would see Lord Walden's evil face and almost every night it had been dawn before she had been able to lose consciousness after tossing and turning and writhing as the memory of him continued to haunt her.

Now she slipped off her gown without feeling agitated, conscious that in some strange way the Marquis had indeed comforted her. And yet what could he do?

He had sworn he would never fight a duel and she believed him. He would not be so foolish as to invite all the scandal and gossip that there would be if he fought a duel at this moment just four days before their Wedding.

There could be only one reason why a Gentleman of Fashion should fire on another and it would be quite obvious that she was involved. But what else could he do?

She found herself turning the question over and over in her mind. Then with a little smile she crept beneath the lavender-scented sheets and remembered that Valdo had always been imaginative.

She could remember when they had been forbidden as a punishment to use the boat on the lake and how he had improvised a raft.

She remembered how once, when she had been forbidden to join him because of some misdemeanour, he carried a ladder round to her window at the Vicarage when everyone was at dinner and persuaded her to climb down and join him in some secret adventure he had planned in the woods.

They had returned after a few hours, Valdo had removed the ladder and no one had been any the wiser about their escapade.

'Valdo will think of something now,' she thought to herself sleepily and, as she slept, his name was on her lips.

The night before when she had been dressing she had instructed her maid to call her at eight o'clock the following morning.

The Dowager had arranged last minute fittings for the Wedding dress and Druscilla had been uneasily aware that there were many letters of thanks still to be written, not only for the many parties that she had attended but also for the

Wedding presents that had been pouring in steadily all through the week.

The Dowager's secretary, Mr. Hanbury, who was also the Comptroller of her household, was a severe grey-haired man whom Druscilla held slightly in awe.

It was not only her own sense of propriety that made her try to keep up to date with the letters but also the feeling that Mr. Hanbury would be shocked and surprised at any omission that she might commit in social courtesies and behaviour.

The Marquis, of course, had been hopeless where the letters were concerned.

"If anyone thinks I am going to write and thank people for all this rubbish," he said, looking at the accumulation of presents in the library, "they are very much mistaken."

"Rubbish!" the Dowager had protested. "How can you be so ungrateful? I have never in my life seen a more delightful collection of gifts."

"Then you write to thank for them, Grandmama," the Marquis said. "I never was much of a hand at writing, in fact I was continually flogged at Eton because my essays were so short and smudged. But write to all these people! Why, the mere thought of it would make me post for the Continent tomorrow night!"

"A reluctant bridegroom!" the Dowager commented with a smile. "Well, I cannot have you upsetting my plans at the last moment, so I presume that Druscilla will have to do what is necessary in the way of thanks."

"I shall put 'Valdo and I are delighted with your gift'," Druscilla suggested, "'but he feels that it is not worth three or four minutes of his precious time'!"

She spoke sarcastically, but her eyes were laughing.

"It's not a man's job," the Marquis expostulated. "I am no conviction about that sort of thing."

"And yet I am certain that your *billets-doux* to a number of fair ladies are very much prized," Druscilla observed.

The Marquis glared at her for a moment and then he laughed.

"I will forgive your impertinence if you will write the letters, Druscilla."

"Very well," she answered him meekly.

"A workman is worthy of his hire," the Dowager said. "It is only an idea, of course, but Druscilla does need a pair of diamond earrings to match her ring."

"Grandmama, you are the original Eve in the Garden of Eden," the Marquis grinned. "Shall I say I will consider it? I might almost add a necklace as my Wedding gift, if I don't have to concern myself with all the bother of the Ceremonial trappings."

"That would certainly be a better salary than I have ever earned in my life before," Druscilla said and he heard the sudden note of seriousness in her voice.

Now Druscilla slipped out of bed and put on the wrapper trimmed with real lace that the Dowager had chosen for her in Bond Street.

She walked to the window, a cup of chocolate in her hand, and looked out on the fluttering greenery of the square.

"It's a lovely day," she said to her maid, who was tidying the room. "I would much rather be riding or driving in Hyde Park than using my pen."

"I hears there are dozens more presents downstairs, miss."

"More?" Druscilla enquired in mock dismay.

She pretended to complain, but it was very thrilling after years of not even getting a Christmas present to find that every knock on the door meant a new gift was arriving.

She knew they were really for the Marquis and yet she would not have been a woman had she not known that even sharing such spoils was excitement itself.

Besides many of the presents were exclusively feminine. Nearly all the Marquis's relations had sent jewellery of some sort.

There were bracelets, brooches, rings and furs, besides handbags, sunshades and trinkets of every type, which could not by any stretch of imagination be meant entirely for the use of the bridegroom.

"Well, if there are more presents," Druscilla said, "the sooner I have finished with this lot of letters the better."

"I'm goin' down to fetch your breakfast, miss," Rose said. "And I'll ask Mrs. Newman just how many there are."

"Yes, do and if Mr. Hanbury unpacks them, as soon as I am dressed I will be able to see them."

"Mr. Hanbury's puttin' them on a list, miss," Rose informed her.

"Yes, I know," Druscilla answered, "and it's a good thing he does so. It would be very awkward if the cards became mixed and I thanked someone for a present they had not sent."

"Yes, indeed, miss."

Rose went from the room and, as Druscilla settled herself at her writing desk, she heard the door behind her suddenly flung open with a crash.

She turned, thinking that her maid must be upsetting the breakfast, only to see to her astonishment that the Marquis was standing in the doorway.

He was still wearing the knee breeches and the pale blue satin coat that he had worn the night before. He looked a trifle dishevelled and for a moment she thought that he must be foxed.

Then she remembered Lord Walden and sprang to her feet. Could there have been – a fight? Had he been – duelling?

Ideas flashed through her mind in a split second and then the Marquis walked forward and she saw that he carried some pieces of paper in his hand,

"There, Druscilla," he announced with a note of triumph in his voice, "there is your revenge!"

As he spoke, he threw the pieces of paper high in the air and they fluttered down, dozens and dozens of them, onto the bed.

Staring at them in perplexity, she saw on each one a signature. It was not difficult for her to recognise the handwriting, the same writing that was on that note which had been waiting for her on her dressing table before she had left Lord Walden's house.

"Just under one hundred thousand pounds," the Marquis said. "Druscilla, do you understand? You will never see him again, he is finished, done for!"

She raised her eyes from the pieces of paper lying on the bed to look at the Marquis.

"Done for?" she asked in a dazed manner.

"He will have to sell his house in London, his horses and I imagine most of his estate. He will never cross your path again, Druscilla, for there is nothing left for him but to stagnate like a turnip in the country."

Druscilla sat down suddenly on the side of the bed. She did not attempt to touch the papers, she could not bring herself to do so.

But she saw them for what they were, notes of hand, I.O.U.'s, and all for varying large amounts of money.

"How did you – manage it?" she asked in a low voice.

"I knew that Walden was a gambler. When I left you, I went back to Devonshire House. I thought it likely that I should find him in the card room, which was exactly where he was "

"But how did you persuade him to play for such high stakes?" Druscilla asked.

"It was not a question of persuading. He was already at the table with three other men, one of them a friend of mine. I told my friend that a certain very lovely lady was waiting to dance with him upstairs. I winked as I spoke and he understood that I wanted his seat. He gave it me. Walden could not refuse to play, indeed why should he? He was not to know that I had overheard your conversation or indeed that you had confided in me."

"No, of course not," Druscilla murmured in a low voice.

"I sat down," the Marquis went on, "and realised that the stakes were beyond my usual touch."

"You might have lost," Druscilla cried.

"Indeed I might," the Marquis replied, "except that Walden was already foxed and I took some precautions to see that he did not sober up."

"How did you do – that?" she enquired.

"Before I entered the room I had a word with one of the servants. I told him to close the windows and make quite certain that his Lordship's glass was kept continually filled."

"That was clever of you," Druscilla commented.

"It was not cheating," the Marquis explained quickly. "I can assure you that there was nothing unconventional in my behaviour. I merely wished to have a clear head myself while his was slightly fuddled."

"He must have been very fuddled to gamble away as much as this," Druscilla said.

The Marquis gave a laugh, but it was not a pleasant sound.

"I admit to needling him a little. No man likes to be thought chicken-livered when it comes to accepting a wager. And luck was with me. Did I not tell you, Druscilla, that if one has confidence it helps when one goes into battle? I was determined that you should be avenged and I knew it was right that you should be. The man facing me was a swine and so I won."

"One hundred thousand pounds!" Druscilla breathed. "That is indeed – a vast sum of money."

"It is to Walden. He is not as wealthy as all that, soft in the pocket or was by no means a man of great fortune."

"Was he upset or angry?" Druscilla asked.

"When I rose from the table," the Marquis answered, "I think then he realised why I was his adversary.

"'The usual two weeks, my Lord?' I asked formally. For the first time he seemed stricken, realising what he had done."

"The others had long since withdrawn from the contest. They had sat at the table fascinated and there had been other spectators drawn by a whisper that here was a contest taking place in which several fortunes were involved."

"And what did – he say?" Druscilla quizzed the Marquis.

"He murmured something, but I had no wish for conversation with him. I turned and walked from the room and then I found that Anthony was following me."

"'You have certainly given Walden a plucking,' he remarked. 'Any particular reason'?"

"Anthony is perceptive, he knew that I would not have stayed up so late or gambled so furiously if there was not something behind it."

"And what did you tell Sir Anthony?" Druscilla asked.

"I said, 'the man is an outsider and a lecher, he deserved it'. But I did not wait to talk to any more people, I wanted to come back to you. I wanted you to know that you are now free."

"*Free!*" Druscilla repeated the word beneath her breath and then she rose from the bed and walked towards the window. "I ought to feel triumphant, but I don't. I just feel relief and in a way rather sorry for his children."

"Forget him, as I said last night, he is no longer of any import in your life."

He looked down at the pieces of paper strewn on the bed.

"I will send someone to collect these," he said almost to himself.

Druscilla turned from the window.

"Valdo, I have something to ask you."

"What is it?" he enquired.

"When he pays up – don't keep that money," she urged, "it is tainted, it is horrible, it is like the sovereign he offered me, which I threw from the window. We don't want it. It might bring us – bad luck."

He smiled at her.

"What do you expect me to do with it?" he asked. "Throw it out of the window into Berkeley Square?"

"No, no, of course not, but I wondered whether you would consider setting up a fund – a Trust – a charity – anything you like to call it?"

"Who for?" he enquired.

"We should have to think of the wording very carefully," Druscilla replied, "but could it not be for gentlewomen who are poverty-stricken and who are in the same position that I was in when I left Lord Walden's house."

The Marquis looked down at the pieces of paper, each of them extremely valuable, each of them a promise to pay what would be a large sum of money to any ordinary person.

Then he looked back at Druscilla.

"Would that please you?"

"It would please me to think that such a fund of money existed to help unfortunate women who are hounded by men such as Lord Walden."

"Then I will tell my Solicitor what to do with the money when I receive it," the Marquis said. "He will contrive something on the lines you have suggested."

"Will you really?" Druscilla enthused. "Oh, thank you!"

"They will thank you in future, those women who have nowhere to go."

"Perhaps we shall save one or two girls like myself," Druscilla said, "who otherwise would have to choose between starvation or a life with some beast of a man."

"You speak as though all men are beasts,"

"Most of them are!" Druscilla answered. "But now I can forget, now I know he is not waiting round every corner – trying to find me."

"I promised you that you would never see him again," the Marquis remarked.

"And I am more grateful – than I can ever say,"

She clasped her hands together and raised her eyes to him. For the first time since the Marquis had come into her bedroom to relate his triumph, it seemed that he became conscious of her red hair streaming over her shoulders and of the diaphanous wrapper that she wore over her thin nightgown.

Just for a moment he looked at her and she felt a sudden twinge of apprehension.

Then he looked away and turned towards the door.

"I am offending all the conventions," he said. "If Grandmama finds me here, I shall be in trouble. Your servant, Druscilla. There is at least one dragon less to destroy."

He was gone before she could answer him.

But for a long time she stood staring at the door, a strange and enigmatic expression in her eyes.

CHAPTER SEVEN

"There are ever so many presents arrived for you, miss," Rose announced excitedly as she brought Druscilla her breakfast tray.

"Oh dear!" Druscilla sighed. "That means more letters of thanks." But quickly she added, "That sounds ungrateful. I am really delighted to have – so many wonderful gifts."

"They are indeed magnificent, miss," Rose agreed with a note of awe in her voice.

Downstairs in the Blue Salon all the presents had been unpacked with the card bearing the giver's name attached to each by a piece of white ribbon.

Druscilla knew that the guests who were to attend the Wedding would be not only curious but critical of the presents that she and the Marquis had received.

She was well aware that the quality of the gifts and the extravagance of many of them were entirely due to the Marquis's station in Society.

She could not help thinking with a wry smile that had she been marrying someone of little import, there would not have been the massive silver plate, the huge candelabra, the gold ornaments or indeed any of the treasures of great value that came pouring into the house hour after hour.

The Dowager's Comptroller, Mr. Hanbury, had listed everything punctiliously, so Druscilla knew it was unlikely that anyone would be offended at being thanked for a gift that they had not sent or have their present ignored by an oversight.

But yesterday evening she had looked with dismay at the long list of letters that she would have to write as soon as they reached Lynche Hall.

At the same time she could not help being rather thrilled at the thought of being in part anyway a recipient of so much largesse.

The Dowager Marchioness's gift had been a manificent diamond necklace.

"This is for you alone," she had said to Druscilla, "and this is your own personal property. If you wish to dispose of it, you can without having all the family Trustees and Solicitors looking down their noses."

"I shall never part with it," Druscilla cried and there were tears in her eyes as she bent to kiss the old lady's cheek. "There is nothing I can give to you in gratitude for all you have done for me – except my heart."

"I thought that belonged to your bridegroom," the Dowager remarked with a cynical note in her voice.

"He must spare you a very large portion of it," Druscilla laughed and then added with a little throb in her voice, "If only you knew what it means to me – to possess anything as sublime and precious as this."

"It will become you. You are very beautiful, my child, but you will be more beautiful still when you become a woman."

Druscilla blushed, knowing full well what she meant.

When she carried the diamond necklace up to her bedroom, she had sat for a long time in front of her mirror, wondering at its sparkle and brilliance and feeling that the mere possession of it healed many of the scars that she had incurred when she had been alone and penniless.

She remembered now that the diamond necklace was still on her dressing table. It would have to go to Carlton House with the other presents, some of which had been despatched the day before.

The Dowager had been half-afraid that, while His Royal Highness was giving the Reception for the bride and bridegroom, he would not wish to be bothered by displaying the Wedding presents that were so essential a part of an ordinary Reception.

But the Prince Regent had been in a good mood when she had broached the question to him.

"But, of course, the presents must be on show," he enthused. "I will set aside the Chinese Room, where they will be displayed to their best advantage. Besides I shall wish people to see what I am presenting to the young couple."

His gift had been a portrait of himself by the artist Lawrence, who he had taken a fancy to.

"Do we really want Prinny's countenance permanently with us?" the Marquis enquired.

"Your children and grandchildren will appreciate it," the Dowager answered. "At least it will show that you were a recipient of the Royal favour. Moreover even if it was not of someone I knew, I should still think it a very fine painting."

Druscilla hoped now that Mr. Hanbury had remembered that she had asked particularly for the Dowager's gift of the diamond necklace to be shown in a prominent position at Carlton House.

'Supposing he has forgotten,' she thought.

It would be easy for anything even as lovely as a diamond necklace to be lost amongst the great mounds of presents that had been carried in coachload after coachload from Curzon Street to Carlton House.

"Give me my wrapper, Rose," Druscilla asked impatiently and, getting out of bed, she slipped her feet into the little white mules trimmed with swansdown that were part of her trousseau.

Rose brought her wrapper from the wardrobe. Of heavy silk trimmed with yard upon yard of *Valenciennes* lace threaded through with narrow velvet ribbons of soft blue, it made Druscilla look very young.

"You're not goin' downstairs like that, miss?" Rose asked.

"Are there many people about?" Druscilla enquired.

"No, indeed, miss. "The Dowager is not yet dressed and most of the staff have already left for Carlton House."

"Then there will not be anyone of importance to see me," Druscilla smiled.

She picked up the diamond necklace in its blue velvet case and ran downstairs to Mr. Hanbury's office. She found him almost knee deep in presents that had just arrived. He was opening them carefully and recording each gift in a large notebook.

"Good morning, Miss Morley," he greeted her and she knew that there was a slight note of surprise in his voice as he observed the way she was robed.

"I have brought you this personally," Druscilla said, holding out the blue case. "I wanted to ask you to make quite sure it goes in the most visible place amongst the presents. It is the one I like best of all."

"I can understand that," Mr. Hanbury said. "They are very fine diamonds."

"I like it not only because it is valuable," Druscilla told him, "but because her Ladyship gave it to me for my very own. I shall treasure it always because – it is mine."

She bent down as she spoke to look at a leather box containing a beautiful gold cup, its handles fashioned with cupids, the engraved plaque in the centre of it showing that it had been given to the Marquis by The Bachelor's Club.

Druscilla laughed.

"I wonder how many will follow his example!" she exclaimed.

"His Lordship has always been a leader of fashion," Mr. Hanbury pointed out.

"Whatever he does, the others do. It's almost childish, is it not?"

"I am sure that everyone is envying his Lordship's good fortune in having found such a beautiful bride," Mr. Hanbury said but with a note of reproof in his voice.

"I thank you, Mr. Hanbury," Druscilla bowed. "I am afraid that I have given you a lot of extra work, but I am very grateful for all the trouble you have taken in listing these gifts. We should never have identified what we have received without your assistance."

"I am only glad that I can be of help, Miss Morley," Mr. Hanbury smiled.

Even as he spoke, the door opened and a footman came in with another parcel on a silver salver.

"This has just arrived from Lynche House, sir," he said to Mr. Hanbury, "with instructions that it must be handed directly to his Lordship. But he has gone ridin' and they are not certain at what time he will return."

"Give it to me," Mr. Hanbury replied, "I will see that his Lordship receives it."

The footman handed it to him and he put it down on his desk.

"You had best list it," Druscilla suggested. "His Lordship has said that he will write no letters of thanks and, if you leave him to open the package, the card is sure to be mislaid."

"I had thought of that myself," Mr. Hanbury said with a little smile. "Shall we see what it is and put it on the list? Then if you wish I can always pack it up again."

"It sounds almost like a conspiracy, does it not?" Druscilla asked. "But I honestly think it would be wiser for you to attach the card to whatever it may be."

"I think so too," Mr. Hanbury agreed.

As he undid the parcel, Druscilla noticed that there was a crest on the red seals that it was adorned with, but it was impossible for her to decipher it.

The paper revealed a black leather ring-box.

Before opening it Mr. Hanbury picked up the card that lay on top of it. He looked at it and Druscilla realised that he was embarrassed.

Before he could speak and indeed before he could lay the card aside, she looked over his shoulder and read what was written.

"*Wear this and I shall know you have not forgotten me.*"

There was no signature, but as far as Druscilla was concerned there was no need for there to be one. While Mr. Hanbury hovered indecisively, she opened the box and saw embedded in the velvet a signet ring set with an emerald.

It was an attractive and expensive gift, but to Druscilla it was a deliberate act of treachery on the part of the Duchess.

Even on her lover's Wedding Day she could not leave him alone, she must thrust out her arms towards him, drawing him to her as surely as if she raised her red lips to his and looked at him with those passion-filled blue eyes.

Druscilla stared at the ring.

Then, closing the case with a snap, she set it down on the table in front of Mr. Hanbury and walked from the room leaving him gazing after her, an expression of dismay on his face.

She went upstairs to her room and somehow the day now seemed dark and drab despite the sunshine outside.

Was she always to be haunted, she wondered, by the women the Marquis had loved and for all she knew still loved?

Was she always to find fair charmers laying traps for him, trying to seduce him, their blue eyes beseeching him for the favours that should in all justice belong to his wife?

And yet why should he consider her? As far as he was concerned, their marriage was simply one of convenience.

She had earned his gratitude by saving him from a duel and she had prevented the Duchess from being involved in a scandal that might have destroyed her socially. That was all!

'What do I get out of it?' Druscilla asked herself.

She knew the answer, knew it in the feel of silk against her skin, in the fragrance of the expensive perfume that scented her hair, in the softness of the bed she had lain on and in the gowns that had filled her wardrobe until they had been packed yesterday for her departure to Lynche Hall.

That was what she was to receive from her marriage – comfort, luxury, a sense of security and a social position that nothing else could have brought her save marriage to one of the most eligible bachelors in the length and breadth of the country.

"Let him have his fun!" she told herself out loud. "I must be very grasping and very mean if after all I have received I grudge him a few hours of amusement with the Duchess, with Bianca de Silva or with any other woman he fancies with fair hair and blue eyes!"

She tried to sound generous and to find a genuine feeling of generosity within herself.

She found to her surprise that she was tense, her fingers clenched together and her eyes not far from tears.

Why, why, why should any gift the Marquis received upset her so much?

It was absurd, it was ridiculous, yet she knew that she hated the Duchess at that moment with a hatred that seemed to sear its way through her body.

The hatred was still with her when hours later she came slowly downstairs in her bridal gown, knowing as the gilt mirrors reflected her progress that she was more beautiful than she had ever imagined that she might be.

'Why should I still be thinking of that tiresome ring?' she asked herself.

Yet she could not help glancing towards the open door of Mr. Hanbury's office.

The presents had now all gone to Carlton House, every one of them. She wondered what he had done with the ring and knew without being told that he would have given it directly into the Marquis's hand as he had been requested to do.

It would not appear amongst the other presents, but he would have received it.

Just for a moment Druscilla stood indecisively in the hall. The carriage was waiting for her outside, her maid was adjusting the train of her dress and the footmen were looking at her with admiration in their eyes.

She could see herself in a mirror.

"You look very lovely, my child," the Dowager had said before she had gone ahead in another coach.

"You look real wonderful, miss!" Rose exclaimed now. "You'll have their eyes startin' out of their heads!"

Quite suddenly the glittering reflection vanished.

Druscilla was only the drab, poorly dressed girl, scared, frightened and without security, running, running, terror-stricken from one place to another with no one to turn to and without even one friend she could put her trust in.

Then with an unconscious lift of her little chin, she walked out through the doorway, across the pavement and into the coach.

The large congregation in St. George's Church, Hanover Square, filled it almost to suffocation.

Never had there been a more fashionable array of elegant gowns, of sparkling jewels, of jangling decorations, of snowy-white cravats and skin-tight satin coats.

It was not only the Marquis who could attract such a distinguished congregation but the fact that the Prince Regent was to be present and would himself give away the bride was enough to make every Statesman, Courtier, Socialite and snob determined to be present.

It was an unprecedented gesture on the part of His Royal Highness and the Marquis was well aware that many people envied him bitterly for this privilege.

It was, of course, the Dowager who had engineered the Royal condescension.

"Your Royal Highness is such an authority on etiquette," she had said to the Prince Regent flatteringly, "I wish to ask your advice."

"But of course," he had replied in delighted tones.

After years of being snubbed and ignored by his father and the dull Court at Buckingham Palace, he was invariably delighted when anyone consulted him, whatever the subject might be.

"Druscilla is an orphan," the Dowager explained. "She has no close relatives and it seems incorrect somehow to invite one of the Lynches to give her away. They are but distant cousins. Who does Your Royal Highness think I should approach?"

The Prince Regent considered this for a moment and then firmly replied,

"The solution is quite obvious, my dear lady, I myself will take her up the aisle."

The Dowager had exclaimed in surprise and gratitude that she was overwhelmed by such a favour.

Only Druscilla knew by the twinkle in her eye and the little twitch at the corner of her mouth that this was what she had intended from the very beginning.

When the Prince Regent appeared in public, he always made an impressive ceremony of it.

Today, despite Royal protocol, he had insisted on arriving before the bride and waiting for Druscilla just inside the porch, which was separated from the congregation by two glass doors.

Although most of them were bored with the social scene, at the same time they would fight ferociously to hold their proper place in the hierarchy of those who were known as the *Bon Ton*.

The Marquis, standing with Sir Anthony beside him at the Chancel steps, was conscious of the whispers and speculative eyes, the jealousy and even the feelings of hatred directed towards him from the fashionable throng.

Glancing over the first few pews he saw many women who had at various times briefly engaged his attention and whose eyes still lingered on him with a fondness and even with a flicker of fire that he knew would burst into flames should he make even the slightest approach towards them.

There were others who looked at him a little wistfully, wishing that he might notice them in passing even for one rapturous night.

There was amongst those waiting an atmosphere of excited anticipation.

There were husbands who loathed him for what they suspected, but who had not sufficient proof to challenge him.

Then in response to some signal the music became louder, the choir burst into song and the glass doors at the end of the Church opened.

The Prince Regent was looking magnificent. This was the type of occasion that he always graced not only with a splendiferous appearance but with originality. His coat of raspberry-pink velvet glittered with decorations.

There were diamonds in the snowy cravat that cascaded down his chest, his white breeches were a poem to his tailor and his coiffure a compliment to his hairdresser.

But it was not at the Prince Regent that the ladies and gentlemen of the congregation gazed, but at the bride on his arm.

Druscilla had intended to take their breath away and she succeeded.

She appeared to be dressed in nothing but diamonds and with dazzling effect as they sparkled in the light of the many candles.

The gown, which clung to her figure, was embroidered all over in diamanté, but original and unheard of before so was her veil.

It framed her small face, making her skin glow with the translucent softness of a pearl and on her head glittered the magnificent diamond tiara that the Marquis had last seen his mother wearing when she attended a Court Ball.

There were diamonds round her neck and on her wrist and instead of the conventional bouquet she carried a snuffbox emblazoned with diamonds and in the centre of it an enamel miniature of the Prince Regent.

Very slowly the Prince Regent and Druscilla processed up the aisle, her long train carried by four small pages in Court dress.

There was a glint in the men's eyes as they watched her, her red hair shining through her veil, her eyes not dropped as was conventional but staring straight ahead. In the women's eyes there was envy, hatred and malice.

How could anyone look so radiant, so lovely and so spectacular that every other member of her sex paled into insignificance beside her?

The Marquis had not been let into the secret of what Druscilla intended to wear and, as she reached his side, she could not help looking up at him and seeing the twinkle in his eyes.

There was no need for him to say,

"Well done!"

They both knew that, if anyone had doubted for a moment why the bachelor Marquis wished to marry, they had their answer at this moment.

Only when the Marriage Ceremony was over, the second when Druscilla had made her vows, did she slip her hand into the Marquis's as they walked towards the Vestry.

Her fingers were cold for it had been an ordeal even though she had not meant it to be. As he took her hand, he bent towards her so that only she could hear what he said.

"You have struck a death blow to every fashionable female in the whole of London," he whispered.

Druscilla gave a little giggle, she could not help it.

Then they were in the Vestry, the Prince Regent was signing the Register and the Dowager was embracing them.

"You are pleased?" she asked the Marquis.

He kissed first her cheek and then her hand.

"You have waved a magic wand, Grandmama. In other times you would have been burnt as a witch."

The Prince Regent went ahead so that he could be at Carlton House first to receive the guests and then, amidst cries and cheers from the crowds outside the Church, the Marquis and Druscilla climbed into the carriage that was to take them to the Reception.

It was the family State coach that the Marquis always used when he attended the Opening of Parliament. A great deal of it was glass, so that the occupants could be seen quite clearly by those who wished to see them.

As the horses trotted down Bond Street, Druscilla and the Marquis bent forward to wave to the people lining the pavement, many of whom had been waiting for many hours to have a glimpse of the bride and bridegroom in what was indisputably the Wedding of the year.

"You look like a star that has fallen out of the sky or shall I say a whole constellation of them!" the Marquis declared.

She turned to smile at him.

"Your Grandmama was determined to give them something to talk about."

"They will indeed talk," the Marquis said. "What did Prinny say when he saw you?"

"He looked quite peevish," Druscilla replied, "and remarked, 'if I had known that you were going to outshine me, I would have put on some more decorations'."

The Marquis threw back his head and laughed.

"That is Prinny all over, he always wants to be the centre of attraction. He does not like playing second fiddle. All the same, Druscilla, you look magnificent."

There was a note of sincerity in the Marquis's voice that made her smile even as she bent forward yet again to wave at another little crowd on the corner of St. James's Street.

"I wonder how long all this junketing will take?" the Marquis asked.

"Bored already?" Druscilla enquired.

"Not particularly," he answered, "but it is always so damn hot at Carlton House. If I had my own way we would leave now for Lynche Hall."

"And miss all the Grace and Favour? How can you be so ungrateful?"

"When you have attended as many crushes as I have at Carlton House," the Marquis said, "you will find them a dead bore."

"That is not the way to speak about your Wedding," she reproached him.

"It is not, is it?" he smiled. "Well, at any rate you will enjoy yourself! What woman does not enjoy a Wedding, especially when it is her own?"

"I certainly think that this is an improvement on our last one," Druscilla replied.

She had a memory of herself in her cheap cotton dress with the hideous old-fashioned bonnet crammed down over her drawn-back hair, her glasses on her nose and the Marquis beside her stiff with fury, his voice hardly under control because of the violence of his feelings.

And then quite clearly she saw the Duchess, her blue eyes misty with tears, her red lips trembling a little.

"How could I have dreamt that the goose-girl would turn out to be a Princess in disguise?" the Marquis asked teasingly.

Druscilla gave a little giggle of laughter.

Suddenly she felt gay and light-hearted, almost as though she had already drunk a glass of the sparkling champagne that would be waiting for them at Carlton House.

"This is certainly a Fairytale Wedding!" she said and there was a note of elation in her voice.

"And, of course, we shall live happily ever after!"

The Marquis spoke quietly and his eyes were serious.

~141~

Druscilla did not know why, but she suddenly felt as if it was hard to breathe and she was blushing.

There was a Reception first at Carlton House and then at five o'clock they sat down to dinner. It was the sort of meal that the Prince Regent loved to arrange. There was every type of delicacy and there were a dozen different wines.

Long before they reached the sorbet halfway through the menu, Druscilla felt that she could eat no more, but the other guests seldom refused a dish.

The footmen with their powdered hair and glittering gold braid brought more and more delectable concoctions on the crested gold plates that Druscilla knew, like everyone else present, had not yet been paid for.

Seated on the Prince Regent's right, she felt as if she was in a dream. Could it be true that she was here, fêted, acclaimed and toasted? Her eyes seemed dazzled by the brilliance of it all.

Then the Prince Regent was whispering in her ear,

"My friend Valdo is a very fortunate fellow. I wish I was to be your bridegroom tonight."

She looked up into his hot pink face, saw the desire in his protruding eyes and was not frightened but amused. Mrs. Fitzgerald, cool, aloof and ladylike at the end of the table was, she knew, sufficient protection.

She felt the Prince's fat fingers squeezing hers and looked at the Marquis on her other side. How clean-cut he looked in contrast.

His broad shoulders, his athletic body without an ounce of spare flesh and the proud carriage of his head made her feel suddenly glad that she had married him.

As if he felt her scrutiny, the Marquis turned towards her and smiled.

Something strange then happened to Druscilla's heart. It was almost as if it turned over in her breast.

He raised his glass to her and something glistened on his little finger.

Druscilla drew in a deep breath.

So he had worn the Duchess's ring!

Today of all days he acknowledged his love for his mistress!

She felt the room go dark, the brilliance dimmed, the magic gone!

She turned to the Prince Regent, her lips deliberately flirtatious.

"What woman would not be honoured and flattered but perhaps also rather – shocked, Sire, at such a suggestion?"

"And you?" he asked. "Are you shocked or flattered?"

"That, Sire, I must leave to your astute imagination."

"You are entrancing!"

The Prince Regent's voice was hoarse.

Druscilla dropped her eyes in mock embarrassment, but her brain was thinking coldly.

'So the Duchess still holds Valdo on a string – he still desires her. But why should I care? There is not and never has been any question of love where we are concerned.'

But she wondered why the future seemed bleak and empty. This was a marriage of convenience with the two people concerned joined together only by social conventions, social amusements and social gossip!

Once she had hoped for a marriage where she would love and be loved. Once she had dreamt of a man, tender and kind, a man at whose touch she would thrill.

But now –

'*I hate all men* – beasts and brutes, they are all animals,' she muttered beneath her breath.

When finally the ladies retired to the drawing room, Druscilla found herself the centre of female flutterings, the target of little barbed arrows that were meant to hurt, of vicious innuendoes and some spontaneous expressions of approval.

"There has never been a more beautiful bride," one woman gushed.

"And she belongs to the Marquis," a fair-haired beauty said crossly. "It's not fair, he has everything."

'Including me,' Druscilla said more to herself than to the assembled throng.

She looked at the gold Wedding ring on her finger. At last she could really believe it.

She was the Marchioness of Lynche and everyone must acknowledge her position, which the poor crushed Governess, who had fought despairingly for respectability, had obtained by chance and by an act of Fate that even now left her breathless to even think about it.

If the Marquis had not come to the schoolroom that night for her help, none of this would have been happening.

She felt that she should sing a song of praise to the skies, but nevertheless, when she drove away in the carriage to Berkeley Square, she was unaccountably depressed.

"I thought we might leave for Lynche Hall tonight," the Marquis said, "but it is too late. We will go tomorrow. I anticipated that we would both be tired after so much eating and drinking and I sent a groom off soon after we arrived at Carlton House to tell them that they could keep their welcoming speeches until after tomorrow."

"Welcoming speeches?" Druscilla enquired.

"But of course," the Marquis said. "Did I not tell you? The staff, the tenants and the villages will all turn out to greet us. There will be ceremonial arches up the drive and I am afraid you will have to shake hands with an enormous number of people. I only hope I can remember who the deuce they all are."

"I had not thought of that," Druscilla muttered quietly.

"If we start off now, it will be very dark before we arrive and it will spoil their fun," the Marquis said. "We will stay in Berkeley Square tonight, that is if you have no objection."

"No, of course not. I will do whatever you please."

"You will find everything you require. I made two plans, one if we stayed in London and one if we went to Lynche Hall, so I think you will be quite comfortable."

"I am sure I shall be," Druscilla responded, remembering how very little comfort had been reserved for her in the past.

The horses stopped outside the house. The red carpet was rolled across the pavement, the Major Domo was just inside the hall with half-a-dozen resplendent footmen.

"May I welcome your Lordship and Ladyship home," he said in stentorian tones, "and on behalf of the staff we wish you every happiness now and in the future."

"Thank you, Granson," the Marquis said. "Please convey to the staff my thanks and those of her Ladyship. I hope you have seen that everything has been arranged for you all to celebrate this auspicious occasion?"

"It has indeed, my Lord. The wine and the fiddlers are upstairs and we were only waiting for your Lordship and Ladyship's return before commencing."

"Don't let us stop you," the Marquis answered. "Would you like a glass of wine or anything to eat, Druscilla?"

"No indeed. At the moment I feel I could never face food again."

She turned and walked up the stairs. She knew her way because she had already seen the Bridal Bedroom at Lynche House, which she knew the Marquis's mother had used when she had been alive.

It was an enchanting room with a large bed set on a dais with silk curtains that fell from a corolla of carved and gilded doves.

Druscilla walked across the room, removing as she did so her tiara from her head. It was heavy and she drew it off with a sense of relief and set it down on the dressing table.

She also took off the glittering shimmering veil, which she well knew had caused more comment than any other fashionable innovation for years.

She threw it over the chair, wondering as she did so why there was no sign of Rose. She turned again towards the dressing table and as she did so heard the Marquis come into the room and close the door behind him.

Then almost before she realised what was happening he had turned her towards him, his arms were round her and he crushed her in his arms.

For a moment she was too surprised to move. His lips were on hers and he was kissing her passionately.

She could not move, she could not cry out.

His mouth, hard and possessive, held her captive and his arms imprisoned her.

For a moment, unable to move, almost unable to breathe, she felt as though it was happening to her in a dream.

He was taking her and possessing her so that she felt as if he drew her very heart from between her lips and made it his.

She could not resist him, she could not escape those fierce demanding kisses and the insistence of his mouth.

She was surrendering herself, giving him what he demanded —

Then, with the sharpness of a knife thrust, she remembered the ring that he was wearing on his finger and the message she had read from the Duchess and knew that his kisses were only like those that other men had forced upon her – kisses of lust and of unbridled passion, but not of love.

As his lips released her mouth to seek the softness of her neck, she fought herself free.

Wildly she ran to the dressing table. She opened the white satin glove box that lay on it, turned round and the Marquis found himself looking into the barrel of a small pistol that she held in her hand.

"Leave me – alone," she gasped, "don't – dare – to touch me."

He stared at her stupefied.

For a moment neither of them spoke.

Then she saw a sudden sparkle of fire in his eyes and knew as he squared his chin and by the twist of his lips that he was very angry.

"How dare you point a gun at me?" he demanded and his voice was like a whip. "I am no Walden to force myself on any woman who is not desirous of my attentions. I assure you, Druscilla, there is no need for dramatics or indeed for such an insult as you are offering me now. Put away your gun, my dear girl. It is quite unnecessary as far as I am concerned for you to possess one."

He stood looking at her and she fancied that there was a cynical contempt in his expression before he said in a voice of icy control,

"I give you my word that I will not touch you again unless you ask me to. You will find that undoubtedly reassuring."

He turned abruptly and walked towards the door.

When he reached it, he looked back.

"I hope, my Lady," and his tone was sarcastic, "that you enjoy your Wedding night. I assure you that I will endeavour to find mine amusing."

He went from the room without closing the door behind him.

Druscilla heard him go down the stairs, heard a murmur of voices in the hall and a door closing.

Only then did the pistol fall from her hand onto the floor. It was not loaded, but she told herself that it had served its purpose.

Then somehow, for no reason she could explain, she began to cry.

She ran across the room and flung herself down on the bed.

She buried her face in the pillows and wept bitterly and forlornly, more lost, lonelier than she had ever been in her whole life – but why?

She did not understand.

CHAPTER EIGHT

After a time Druscilla stopped crying, but she lay still with her face in one of the pillows.

She thought of the anger on the Marquis's face, of the expression in his eyes and of the sarcastic and cynical note in his voice as he bade her 'goodnight'.

She could still feel the pressure of his lips on hers, but she was still quivering under the passion beneath his kiss and the possessiveness that seemed to suck her strength from her and leave her limp in his arms.

And yet she now knew to her surprise and for some extraordinary reason that she did not understand that she had not been frightened.

From the first moment when he had taken her in his arms and crushed her against him she had felt weak and helpless and had no desire to fight him.

Then she remembered the glitter on his finger as he had raised his glass to her at Carlton House.

It was the memory of that which had made her fight for her freedom and sent her rushing to the glove box on her dressing table to seek the pistol that she had bought the first day after she had arrived in London.

Even under the Dowager's protection she had thought that Lord Walden might seek her out.

She had discovered the name of a gunsmith and, evading the surveillance of her great-aunt, she had gone there alone to purchase a weapon, which she hoped would frighten Lord Walden if nothing else.

"And what can a young Lady of Fashion like yourself want with such a dangerous weapon?" the gunsmith had asked her.

Druscilla knew that he was being familiar because she had come into the shop unaccompanied.

"I may be going abroad," she had replied coldly, "and I am told that there are many bandits and robbers on the continent."

It was the natural authority in her voice rather than the explanation that made him more subservient.

Finally she purchased a small pistol, ivory-handled and small enough to be concealed in a muff or a reticule, but nevertheless when loaded it was a weapon that could, if properly aimed, kill a man.

Druscilla had forgotten about it in the days that followed until, after her encounter with Lord Walden at Devonshire House, she looked to see if it was still where she had placed it in the satin box that stood on her dressing table.

When the Marquis had told her that Lord Walden would not be seen in London again, she had not given another thought to the pistol lying amongst her gloves until tonight.

She wondered now, lying on the bed and crumpling the glittering brilliance of her Wedding gown, why she had suddenly remembered its existence.

As a weapon it had certainly proved effective. It had driven her bridegroom away from her, perhaps forever.

"I hate him," she called out aloud, "I hate him, *I hate him.*"

She wondered why she felt so little elation at the fact that he had left her and gone in search of a more amenable female.

Undoubtedly Bianca de Silva would welcome him with open arms and laugh to see how little marriage had severed him from his old habits.

*

It was laughter that Druscilla feared the following morning when after a sleepless night Rose called her with her breakfast at nine o'clock.

She was well aware that Rose and all the rest of the household would know that the Marquis had not stayed with her but had left the house soon after they returned from Carlton House.

She knew how such a titbit of gossip would sweep through the house from the upper servants down to the scullions and pantry boys. Everyone would know and everyone would gossip about it.

She had lived recently too close to the servants' hall not to know the type of remark that would be made, the sniggers that would follow and then the coarse speculation as to what had occurred.

She felt humiliated, but she recognised that it was really her sense of insecurity that made her suffer.

Had she been truly aristocratic and born into the life that she now found herself in, the servants' chatter would have been of no consequence to her.

She knew that Rose's eyes were on the uncreased pillow beside her and she forced herself with an effort to speak quietly and casually of the weather as the maid tidied the room.

Although the sunlight flooded in through the window, it seemed in some extraordinary way to bring no brightness with it.

"I don't need any breakfast," Druscilla said and her voice was tired. "Please take the tray away."

"My Lady, you'll feel ever so fatigued if you don't eat," Rose expostulated. "You have a long coach drive ahead of you."

"Yes, of course, we are leaving for Lynche Hall this morning," Druscilla replied. "Have you any idea what time his Lordship wishes to depart?"

There was silence for a moment and, when Rose answered, Druscilla knew that she was embarrassed.

"His Lordship has not yet returned."

"Returned?" Druscilla questioned involuntarily.

"His Lordship did not sleep here last night."

It was like a slap in the face and yet Druscilla knew that she might have expected it.

She had driven him to it, she thought, with a self-honesty that could not be denied, she had driven him from his own house on his Wedding night and she had no one to blame but herself.

If he had not worn that ring and if he had not flaunted in front of her his infatuation for the Duchess, everything might have been different.

And yet would it?

Could she really have endured his kisses and the touch of his hands? She asked herself that question and did not know the answer.

She could see nothing but the glint of the ring as he had raised his glass in silent toast, his eyes looking towards her with an expression that she felt was one of admiration. And yet she could not be entirely sure.

She realised that Rose was waiting for her to speak and after a moment she said quietly,

"We must just wait until his Lordship returns. I daresay he had made plans. They are waiting to celebrate our Wedding at Lynche Hall."

"Yes, my Lady," Rose agreed, "and the Major Domo has suggested that the baggage coach I am to travel in should leave at half an hour before eleven o'clock, if that will suit your Ladyship."

"Yes of course, Rose," Druscilla nodded. "I will rise now."

"I thought your Ladyship would wear your new drivin' coat with the tiered cape. The blue is vastly becomin'."

"Yes, bring me that and the blue gown," Druscilla answered. "I would wish those at Lynche Hall to see me looking my best."

She rose, bathed and dressed slowly. Every moment she expected a message to tell her that the Marquis had returned, but there was no message.

Finally, when she was ready, she stood for a moment staring at her reflection in the mirror, not seeing how the pale forget-me-not blue of the coat and bonnet became her, but only the troubled darkness of her own eyes, which seemed to hold questions that she could not answer.

"Finish the packing, Rose," she commanded, "you must not be late for the baggage coach."

"No indeed, my Lady, and I thinks we shall not be far behind your Ladyship in case you have need of me."

"I will manage until you get there," Druscilla said. "It does not take more than two hours to drive to Lynche Hall, so his Lordship has informed me."

"Yes, my Lady."

Rose dropped a curtsey.

Druscilla went from the room and walked slowly down the staircase to the hall.

She felt as though there were eyes everywhere watching her progress, eyes from curious housemaids, eyes from obsequious footmen and eyes from the Lynche ancestors that hung in gilt frames covering the walls of the hall and the staircase.

'How could Valdo do this to me?' she asked herself.

She knew that it was a subtle revenge for the hurt that she must have inflicted on him last night, a hurt not so much to his heart as to his pride.

She reached the hall and just as she did so the knocker rapped on the front door. She turned her face towards it expectantly.

Could this be the Marquis returning? But instead she saw Mr. Hanbury enter.

"Good morning, Mr. Hanbury," she said, glad to have someone to speak to. "I am delighted to see you, because this gives me an opportunity – to thank you for all the arrangements you made at Carlton House yesterday.

Everything went off most smoothly and efficiently and I know it was all due to your most excellent organisation."

For the first time since she had known him Mr. Hanbury s rather sad face lightened.

"You are indeed gracious, my Lady," he murmured. "I myself was pleased that there was no hitch in the proceedings."

"No indeed," Druscilla said.

They moved a little way into the hall as they were speaking and now Druscilla glanced down and saw that he held a small square leather case in his hand.

She stared at it, knowing that she had seen it before and that it was the box that Mr. Hanbury had opened in her presence the day before containing the ring from the Duchess.

Mr. Hanbury saw her glance and looked embarrassed.

"You must forgive me, my Lady," he said, "but I did not expect to find you here. I brought this Wedding gift to place in the safe keeping of the Marquis's Comptroller."

Druscilla did not speak and after a moment he went on in a most apologetic tone,

"You will think it exceedingly remiss of me, my Lady, especially after your kind words, but this gift for the Marquis escaped my memory. When I left you yesterday morning, I had every intention of taking it with me to Carlton House and of presenting it to the Marquis at a suitable opportunity. Most regrettably I forgot. It was extremely reprehensible of me, but I hope that your Ladyship will understand."

Druscilla stared at him, her eyes wide.

"You – mean," she said, stammering a little over the words, "that you did not give – his Lordship the ring that – came to him from the Duchess?"

"No, my Lady," Mr. Hanbury confessed. "I am afraid I put the box in my pocket and I only discovered it last night when I retired to bed."

His tone of voice was slightly evasive and Druscilla knew in that moment that he had acted deliberately.

Knowing, as was inevitable, of the liaison between the Duchess and the Marquis, he had held back her gift until after the Wedding was over.

It was a deliberate act of kindness and yet now, almost like a schoolboy caught out in an act of mischief, he was ashamed of his interference.

"I don't – understand," Druscilla said in a low voice. "His Lordship was wearing an emerald ring – yesterday. I saw it myself."

"Yes, indeed, my Lady. The Marquis was wearing the Lynche betrothal ring. It is customary for the Head of the Family to wear that ring on the occasion of his nuptials."

"But it is an emerald," Druscilla insisted.

"Yes, it is an emerald," Mr. Hanbury repeated firmly, "but a very much finer specimen than this one. It belongs to the collection that your Ladyship wore the night of the party given by her Ladyship at Curzon Street."

Druscilla's eyes were on his and, pleased to be able to impart information, he continued,

"The Lynche emeralds, which as you know are historic and very famous, were acquired by the first distinguished member of the family, Sir Robert Sloan, who was one of the great adventurers in the reign of Queen Elizabeth. They were part of the spoils he took from a Spanish ship he captured in the West Indies. When he brought the emeralds back to England, they were made into a magnificent set for his wife and one of the purest and most valuable of the stones into a ring for himself. He wore the ring on his Wedding Day and since then each subsequent Head of the Family has maintained the tradition."

'So it was not the Duchess's ring that Valdo had been wearing!'

Druscilla was not certain if she said the words aloud or merely spoke them in her heart. She only knew that she felt as though the hall was whirling around her dizzily.

She could not be sure whether she was relieved or humiliated by her mistake or only angry that the Duchess had once again managed to disrupt the Marquis's life.

But how could she have known, how could she have imagined for one moment that there were two emerald rings – one on the Marquis's finger, the other in the box that Mr. Hanbury had so tactfully forgotten so that the gift should not disturb her Wedding Day?

She realised that Mr. Hanbury was waiting. He was anxious and a little alarmed lest what he had done had incurred her displeasure.

She laid her hand on his arm.

"Thank you," she said softly, "I am grateful."

Then she turned away and walked into the library at the far end of the hall.

It was a long room overlooking a small paved garden at the back of the house where a fountain was playing. Sunshine was streaming through the windows, shining on the Persian rugs and lighting the walls covered from floor to ceiling by shelves filled with books.

It was a beautiful room with a great carved gilt mirror over the mantelpiece and French furniture brought to England by a Lynche who had been Ambassador to Paris at the time of the French Revolution.

But Druscilla saw only the emptiness of it.

She walked to the window to look outside, but she really was concerned only with the tumult within herself.

What had she done by her hasty action in driving the Marquis from her, striking at him because the wounds she had suffered in the past made her behave in what now seemed a foolish even hysterical manner?

Why could she not have asked him why he wore the Duchess's ring and thus discovered for herself that he had no knowledge that such a ring had even been given to him?

She knew now that in some way she had been afraid, afraid of surrendering her body to a man, but if she must do so, then she would rather it was Valdo than any other man in the world.

She remembered how she had adored him as a boy. Had he really changed so much? Was it really necessary for her to threaten him with a pistol to drive him from her side?

She thought despairingly that once again she found herself in an impossible situation, once again she was caught in an emotional tangle that it was hard to see a way of escape from.

'Fool! *Fool!*' She felt that the clock ticking on the mantelpiece was repeating the word over and over again.

'*Fool, fool!*' to be so impetuous and so impulsive as not to have discovered the truth before acting so violently.

The door behind her opened and she turned eagerly.

It was only the Major Domo.

"His Lordship has sent a message, my Lady."

"A message?" Druscilla queried. "Then he is not – here?"

"No, my Lady. His Lordship asks that you should go ahead in the coach, which is waiting outside. He will follow in his high perch phaeton and will meet your Ladyship at *The Crown and Feathers*, which is a Posting inn about three miles from Lynche Hall. You will then be able to arrive together to receive the welcome of those who are awaiting your presence."

Druscilla drew in a deep breath. Just for a moment she wanted to scream that she would not travel to Lynche Hall without the Marquis, she would not drive alone and be humiliated in front of the staff by such a decision.

Then she knew that it would only make things worse if she refused to leave or indeed argued about it.

"I will do as his Lordship wishes," she said quietly.

"I have arranged a glass of wine and a sandwich for your Ladyship," the Major Domo said suavely. "There will doubtless be a light repast waiting for you at *The Crown and Feathers*, but your Ladyship might care to partake of something now."

Druscilla knew that he meant it kindly, so to please him she sipped at a glass of wine and nibbled the corner of one sandwich.

She felt as though the food would choke her, but she was concerned only with behaving with dignity while striving to give the appearance of not being perturbed by the instructions from a bridegroom who had not slept in the house on his Wedding night.

Finally, walking across the hall, she saw that the red carpet had been laid across the pavement and a coach was waiting outside.

It was a new coach, which the Marquis had bought quite recently and which had been built for speed. It was well sprung and drawn by four horses, which he liked to tool himself.

There were two coachmen on the box wearing smart tiered capes and high hats and there were two outriders both mounted on spirited horseflesh.

Druscilla realised that this was a way of conveying the Marquis's riding horses from London to Lynche Hall.

The outriders, with their powdered wigs, blue and yellow uniforms and polished boots, were part of the elegance of the whole cavalcade.

Only when she was seated against the soft-cushioned back and her knees were covered with an ermine rug did she realise how lonely it was to drive away by herself with no one at her side.

The Major Domo, standing on the pavement, bowed as she left, as did all the footmen behind him.

Druscilla was quite sure that there would be peeping eyes from all the windows upstairs and that people in the street turned to stare as they trotted round the square and started driving through the traffic towards the outskirts of London.

To reach Lynche Hall they travelled for a long way on the main route to Dover, so the coach moved at a good pace. Druscilla began to wonder how long she would have to wait before Valdo caught them up in his high perch phaeton.

He could proceed faster, but he would have to leave not more than three quarters of an hour later if he was to arrive at *The Crown and Feathers* at more or less the same time.

'Supposing he has no intention of doing so?' a cynical and mocking voice within her asked.

This could be a subtle way of punishing her by making her wait at a small and scruffy inn until her husband was ready to leave his paramour who he had doubtless spent the night with.

Druscilla put her hand up to her face. She was past tears, but she was terribly apprehensive of the future.

She longed to see the Marquis and yet at the same time she dreaded to encounter once again the expression that she had seen on his face the night before.

The coach had been travelling for nearly an hour and they were out in the open countryside with hardly a house in sight when suddenly without any warning whatsoever there was a shout and the horses were pulled to a standstill.

For a moment Druscilla could not imagine what had occurred.

Then, even as she bent forward to look out of the open window, the doors of the coach were flung open on either side and she faced two pistols pointing at her held in the hands of men who were both masked.

She wanted to scream, but her voice died in her throat.

The word 'highwaymen' flashed before her eyes in letters of fire.

One pistol was pointed at her breast, but the man on the other side of the coach seemed disconcerted that there was no one in the seat beside her.

He stared at the empty place and then pulled at the rug as though he half-expected to find someone crouching beneath it.

"'E ain't 'ere."

The man's voice was low, hoarse and uneducated.

As suddenly as they had come, they went. They slammed the two doors of the coach and Druscilla was alone again.

Unable to understand what was happening she saw through the window the outriders each holding one hand shoulder high, while they controlled their restless horses with the other.

There was a highwayman in front of each of them, masked and with pistols pointed ominously. There were two other men with their weapons trained on the coachmen.

They all seemed to be waiting for something and Druscilla could see that the two men on foot who had opened the coach doors were now running up a small incline on the roadside, where after a second or two they were effectively hidden by the green branches of the trees.

Six highwaymen! Who had ever heard of so numerous a band of outlaws?

Then Druscilla sensed that Eustace was responsible for this.

Only Eustace would have known that there would be two coachmen on the box and two outriders, four men to cope with as well as the Marquis had he been there.

Only Eustace would have planned such a grandiose operation.

Highwaymen usually worked the roads by themselves or with one fellow felon at most. Had there been a gang of six operating so near London, troops would have been sent to disperse them before now.

No, these were not highwaymen, Druscilla realised that. They were criminals hired by Eustace to kill Valdo and then disappear so that no one would be able to trace them.

She could see all too clearly how Eustace had planned it. The men would have jerked open the door of the coach, the Marquis would have reached for his pistol had he carried one and they would have shot him down beside her.

There would have been nothing that the coachmen or the outriders could do about it. Six men with intent to murder against five journeying peacefully along the King's highway was something that no one could have anticipated, not even the Marquis.

Druscilla kept her eyes on the wood that the two men on foot had disappeared into. For a few seconds nothing happened and then one of them appeared.

He called out something, gesticulated and his four confederates on horseback turned their mounts and rode away.

The fact that it was so surprising and quietly done was sinister in itself.

The coachmen whipped up the horses, the outriders lowered their hands and they were off again and moving, Druscilla knew, at an unprecedented speed and driven by a quite understandable desire to get away before the highwaymen changed their minds.

After waiting until the coach had proceeded perhaps half a mile, she called to the coachmen to draw up. They obeyed her, but reluctantly, feeling that they were not yet far enough away from the scoundrels who could easily overtake them.

The coachman who was not driving climbed down.

"We should hurry on, my Lady," he said to Druscilla. "Those men may still pursue us. Did they take anythin' belongin' to your Ladyship?"

"They took nothing," Druscilla answered. "And you need not be alarmed, they will stay where they are. It was not me they were seeking."

"Yes, my Lady," the coachman said, obviously ill at ease.

"Is there an inn near here?" Druscilla asked.

"There is a small one not a few hundred yards away," the man replied. "'Tis not much of a place, but I sees it now in the distance."

"Stop there," Druscilla ordered him.

The coach drew up at the inn. By that time Druscilla had made her plans and she stepped out of the coach.

"I have a feeling," she began, "that those men intended to rob his Lordship. I intend to go back and warn him."

"My Lady, that's impossible," the coachman expostulated.

"Not at all," Druscilla answered. "Find out if the landlord has a side-saddle with a pommel – and hurry."

The servant looked at her as if he thought she was deranged. At the same time he had been brought up to obey the commands of the quality, however strange they might seem.

It was only a few minutes before a side-saddle was produced.

"Put it on that horse," Druscilla said, pointing to a bay that one of the outriders was riding.

It was a spirited animal with a touch of Arab in him. She turned to the publican of the inn, who was bowing almost to the floor at the honour of receiving such a noble guest at his poor hostelry.

"Have you a wife?" Druscilla asked him.

"Yes, my Lady, she is within."

Druscilla walked into the house that was low-ceilinged, poorly equipped and slightly smelly. A pleasant-looking woman wearing a mob cap dropped her a curtsey.

"Have you a pair of scissors or a sharp knife?" Druscilla asked.

"A sharp knife, ma'am, yes, indeed," the woman replied, surprised and flustered at the same time.

Druscilla pulled up the skirts of her driving coat.

"I want you to cut my dress open from the hem to above the knee at the back," she said.

The woman gave a cry.

"Oh, ma'am, such lovely material!"

"Please do as I say – and quickly," Druscilla urged.

The woman took a long sharp knife, which had doubtless been used for carving meat and chickens for the table.

She then hacked away at the thin gauze of the skirt, which cut easily.

"Thank you," Druscilla said.

She walked outside, while the woman stood looking after her in a bewildered fashion, and found that the horse was already saddled.

She pulled off her bonnet and threw it on the floor of the coach and, taking a chiffon scarf from around her neck, she tied it over her head.

"Help me into the saddle," she asked.

She heard the skirt of her dress tear further as she put her leg over the pommel, but any impropriety was concealed by the full skirt of her riding coat, which covered one side of her and spread out over the horse's back.

She turned to the coachman,

"Drive on to *The Crown and Feathers* and wait there for his Lordship and myself. If we are not there by the time it is dark, drive on to Lynche Hall."

"Very good, my Lady," the coachman said respectfully, but unable to disguise the critical look in his eyes.

He thought she was crazy and she was not at all sure that he was not right. She turned to the remaining outrider, who was still mounted,

"Come with me," she said and they set off back towards London.

Druscilla left the road almost immediately. They rode across country through several fields and then turned parallel with the road, keeping the wood where the highwaymen had hidden on their right.

There was always the risk that they would see her, but she dare not allow too long a time to elapse before they rejoined the main road.

She reckoned that the Marquis would still be some way behind her, even if he left punctually so as to be at *The Crown and Feathers* by the time of her arriving. But she could not be sure.

When finally she joined the main road, she looked anxiously Westwards, half-afraid that she might see a high perch phaeton speeding towards that sinister dark wood in which lurked six men intent on murder.

There was no sign of anything save for two mail coaches and she turned almost light-heartedly towards London, travelling so fast that the outrider had some difficulty in keeping up with her.

When they reached the outskirts of the City, she drew her horse to a standstill.

"I want you to stay here," she said to him. "His Lordship might come a different way out of the City. It is unlikely, but we must take no chances. Here, where the Dover road begins, wait and if you see him tell him what has happened."

"Very good, my Lady," the man answered. "Will your Ladyship be safe alone?"

"I shall be safe – but be sure to keep a careful watch. I assure you that those men are waiting for his Lordship and – should you fail to warn him his death will be on your hands."

There was a little tremor in her voice as she spoke.

Then she was moving swiftly away to where the houses became more frequent and there was quite a lot of traffic. People looked at Druscilla curiously, but she thought of one thing and one thing only – to reach the Marquis and warn him of the latest plot conceived in Eustace's mad mind.

On and on she went, but to her consternation there was no sign of the Marquis. Once or twice she saw a high perch phaeton and her heart gave a leap of relief only to find that it was being tooled by someone very different from the man she was seeking.

Finally, without having had a glimpse of the Marquis, she arrived at Berkeley Square.

The door was open because a footman was in the process of taking in a parcel.

He stared up at her in astonishment.

"Has his Lordship been here?"

At the sound of her voice an older and more responsible footman came from the interior of the house. He glared at her and then went quickly inside obviously to fetch the Major Domo.

It was only a few seconds before the Major Domo, an elderly man who Druscilla knew had been in the Lynche service for over thirty-five years, came hurrying across the pavement.

"My Lady, what has happened?" he asked in tones of alarm.

"Where is his Lordship?" Druscilla enquired.

"His Lordship has not been here," the man replied, "the phaeton is meeting him elsewhere."

"Where is that?" Druscilla asked.

The Major Domo hesitated and she said sharply,

"Don't be a fool, man. His Lordship's life is in danger and I have to warn him. What is Miss de Silva's address?"

The surprise on the Major Domo's face was plain to see, but, because of the urgency of her tone, he did not prevaricate.

"It's not far, my Lady, 24 Half Moon Street."

"I know where it is," Druscilla said and trotted away before he could say anything more.

She found her way without difficulty to Half Moon Street. The road, comprising small upright houses, had, Druscilla knew, a doubtful reputation, being favoured not only by expensive ladies of easy virtue but also by a large number of rakish bachelors.

As she turned into the street, she saw with a sinking of her heart that there was no sign of the Marquis's phaeton.

Indeed the street was almost empty save for a curricle drawn up at the far end and a rather disreputable-looking phaeton that could not under any possible circumstances have been one of the Marquis's vehicles.

She dismounted with a little difficulty outside number 24 and saw a small ragged boy playing in the gutter.

"Hold my horse," she commanded him and he ran delightedly to do as she asked.

She rapped on the door. After a few moments it was opened by an elegant, theatrically dressed maidservant who looked at her with an insolent expression.

"Miss de Silva ain't at home," she said before Druscilla could speak.

"Is the Marquis of Lynche – here?" Druscilla enquired.

"I have no idea," the maid replied. "That's not my business and it's not yours."

Druscilla stepped past the woman into the narrow hallway. She saw a high hat on the table at the foot of the stairs.

It might be the Marquis's, but she was not sure. All top hats looked the same.

Without speaking to the maidservant she started to climb the stairs.

The woman gave a cry.

"'Ere, you can't do that."

She would have come after Druscilla, but she remembered that she must shut the door and by the time she had done so Druscilla had already passed the first floor and was climbing the stairs to the second.

She guessed that the main bedroom would be in the front. The door was closed, but she knocked on it loudly.

For a moment there was no answer and then a woman's voice almost screamed,

"Who is it?"

Before Druscilla could reply the door was opened and the Marquis stood there. He must have just been leaving because he was fully dressed.

He stared at Druscilla incredulously and then as a voice yelled from the bed again, "who is it?" the Marquis found his tongue.

"Druscilla, what the Devil are you doing here?" he demanded in furious tones.

"I have come to warn you," Druscilla replied.

For a moment he looked at her and seemed to take in her hair straggling untidily from beneath the tightly tied chiffon scarf, her pale blue coat creased and crumpled, her general air of agitation and the seriousness of her expression.

He stepped out into the passage, closing the door behind him.

"You should not have come here," he said reprovingly, "you know that."

"What does it matter?" Druscilla asked sharply. "Eustace has six highwaymen, or rather six murderers, waiting for you on the Dover Road. You will not have a chance if you go that way. I rode back to warn you."

He looked at her in silence.

"I had to find out for certain – where you were," Druscilla continued and even to herself her voice sounded weak and ineffective. "I went to Berkeley Square and they told me that your phaeton had left. There was no sign of it – outside."

She knew that there was no need to offer him an explanation and yet somehow she was unable to prevent herself from giving him one.

"The groom is walking the horses," he said abruptly.

He made a gesture for her to precede him down the stairs.

She walked down ahead of him, conscious for the first time of how untidy she must look, conscious of his disapproval and conscious too that, as he had opened the door, she had seen a lovely face framed by fair hair lying against the pillows of an ornate bed.

The insolent maidservant opened the door for them. There was a smile on her lips as though she was relishing the thought that there had been a row.

The Marquis picked up his hat and they walked out into the sunshine. Druscilla's horse was standing quite quietly, being patted by the small ragged boy.

Druscilla had ridden fast and it was not as skittish as it had been when they had first left London.

Even as they emerged onto the pavement, the high perch phaeton came from Curzon Street, the chestnuts driven by the Marquis's groom.

"What are you going to do?" Druscilla asked him.

She tried to speak dispassionately, but her voice trembled.

"I do not see why Eustace should prevent us reaching Lynche Hall," the Marquis said angrily. "*Damn him* for his interference! We cannot put the celebrations off for a second time."

"Is there another road?" Druscilla asked,

"Not without taking a very much longer time to reach Lynche Hall," the Marquis replied.

He glanced down at her and for the first time it seemed to Druscilla that some of the coldness and disapproval had gone from his expression.

"Are you too tired to ride there?" he asked.

She felt her spirits revive as though someone had given her a glass of champagne.

"Of course not," she answered. "The coach will be waiting for us – at *The Crown and Feathers*. We can meet with them there and – no one at Lynche Hall need know what has happened."

"Then that is what we will do," the Marquis said. "I imagine you would like to change into a riding habit."

"I hope there is one at Lynche House," Druscilla replied, "but I am not sure."

"Well, we must certainly go and find out," the Marquis said, helping her into the high perch phaeton and telling the groom to ride Druscilla's horse.

Druscilla was not surprised when they reached Berkeley Square to see that the Major Domo was waiting for them on the pavement. He must have guessed that they would return together.

The Marquis gave him no chance to speak.

"I require luncheon and two of my best horses from the stable. Her Ladyship will ride one and I shall ride the other."

"Very good, my Lord "

Druscilla started to ascend the stairs. She heard the Major Domo tell one of the footmen to inform the housekeeper that her Ladyship needed her immediately.

She went up to the room where she had slept the night before.

She felt that what lay in the drawer accused her wordlessly.

Then she realised that, if she had not driven the Marquis away and if they had left as they had planned for Lynche Hall that morning, then by now Valdo would have been dead. Eustace would have killed him and become the new Marquis of Lynche.

'I have saved him,' she said to herself, 'saved him once again!'

Then, almost by some fantasy and magic, she thought that she heard Eustace laugh.

It was the wild insane laughter of a man who is convinced that he will triumph in the end and she seemed to hear him say, almost as though he said it in her ear,

"Third time lucky!"

CHAPTER NINE

Druscilla entered the salon knowing that she was looking her best.

As she had hoped, Rose had left a riding habit behind in Berkeley Square. Druscilla had not worn it before and it would have been far too smart and fashionable in the country.

It was indeed intended only for riding in Hyde Park, but she realised that it became her almost more than anything else she possessed.

Of pale green velvet, the tight-fitting coat was fragged with darker green braid and was fastened with tiny round buttons of sparkling green stones.

Druscilla did not put on her hat but carried it in her hand. High and cone-shaped, it was bound with a floating veil of green gauze that matched the velvet of her habit.

She came into the room with a little smile on her face wondering if she would see a look of admiration in the Marquis's eyes.

But with the thought she remembered the face that she had seen against the pillow, a lovely petulant face framed with fair hair and a naked shoulder peeping above the bedclothes.

Resolutely she tried to put the memory from her and walked towards the Marquis, who was standing by the fireplace with a smile on her lips. He did not look at her, he only drew his watch on its fob from his waistcoat pocket and said abruptly,

"We should start as soon as possible. I would not wish to keep the welcoming committee waiting for a second time."

'He is angry!' Druscilla thought dismally.

She knew only too well the sharp note in his voice and the way he tightened his lips when he was incensed.

She felt her spirits sink.

During her ride towards London, when she had been distraught with anxiety for his safety, she had almost forgotten his anger of the night before.

'I must tell him that I made a mistake about the ring,' she told herself.

But she knew that to explain it would be extremely embarrassing for how could she confess that she had read the private message that the Duchess had written for his eyes alone?

She recalled how irritated the Marquis had been on the previous occasion when she had intercepted a message that she thought had come from the Duchess, but in reality had been the first of Eustace's attempts at murder.

"Kindly allow me to manage my own affairs, Druscilla," he had said and now she felt it was unlikely that he would welcome another example of what he would consider her interfering ways.

'Yet somehow I must make him understand that I am sorry,' Druscilla reflected as they walked towards the dining room.

"I have ordered a small collation, which we must eat quickly," the Marquis said in what she recognised as a commanding voice.

It must have been, she thought, the way he spoke to the troops when he was directing them in battle.

"Yes, of course," she agreed meekly.

She seated herself at the table and helped herself from the first dish that was offered to her.

She suddenly realised that she was feeling hungry.

The long ride to London had given her an appetite to enjoy the food that she ate, but she noted that the Marquis waved away most of the dishes he was offered and seemed to nibble only tentatively at some cold brawn, almost as if the mere sight of food nauseated him.

She saw the dark lines under his eyes and thought that he had spoken the truth when he had claimed that he would amuse himself on his Wedding night.

She longed to ask him what he had done and where he had been, but even as the question formed itself in her mind she realised how stupid she was. It was obvious who he had spent the night with.

She was amazed at the stabbing pain, almost like the thrust of a dagger, that the knowledge gave her.

They ate in silence. Then, while Druscilla would still have liked to sample one of the huge hothouse peaches that she knew had been sent to London from Lynche Hall, the Marquis rose to his feet.

"I regret having to inconvenience you in any way," he said formally, "but I think we should start our journey without further delay."

"Yes, of course," Druscilla agreed.

She did not keep him waiting by going upstairs again.

She put on her hat in front of one of the mirrors in the hall, noting as she did so that the housemaid who had waited on her in Rose's absence had arranged her hair most attractively and so skilfully that it was unlikely to become dislodged however hard she rode.

Outside in the sunshine two spirited horses were waiting for them. The groom helped Druscilla into the saddle.

Her velvet skirt was arranged over the pommel and fell gracefully over the stirrup. She might have been going for a quiet outing in Hyde Park, but she knew that there was a hard ride ahead of them and was glad that she felt so well.

The food and a glass of wine had revived her spirits and she thought that somehow she would contrive to coax the Marquis out of his fit of the sullens and have him laughing with her again.

She remembered the look that he had given her at the dinner at Carlton House when he had raised his glass to her in a silent toast.

There had been something in his eyes that made her suddenly breathless and yet at the same time made her heart throb so violently that she could feel it beating tumultuously within her breast.

Then she had seen the ring on his finger. How was she to know, she asked herself despairingly, that there were two emerald rings and that he had never received the one sent him by the Duchess?

'It will be all right – I *know* it will be all right,' Druscilla repeated to herself.

Equally she could still see the anger in the Marquis's eyes when he faced the pistol she held in her hand and hear the cynical bitterness in his voice.

"We must not forget to collect the groom on our way," she said aloud as they turned their horses towards the Dover road.

"I shall not forget," the Marquis replied, "but we had best make as good a speed as we can once we are out of this cursed traffic."

The tone of his voice was irritable and she guessed that he had a headache. This was not the moment for reconciliation.

In any case there was now no possibility of conversation.

The Marquis forced the pace and apart from stopping a few seconds while they collected the groom, they rode hard and without respite until they reached *The Crown and Feathers*.

The Head Coachman was standing outside the inn looking anxiously up the road as they arrived.

"I'm real glad to see your Lordship!" the man exclaimed as they drew their sweating mounts to a standstill.

"Stable these horses, Jarvis," the Marquis ordered, "and we will leave immediately. Is the coach ready?"

"Ready this half-hour, my Lord," Jarvis replied proudly. "I reckoned your Lordship would be arriving about now, that was if her Ladyship had to ride as far as London."

"I was just on the point of leaving," the Marquis said shortly and turned towards the coach.

The grooms were holding the horses, which having been rested and fed were impatient to move off.

The Marquis stood back to let Druscilla enter the coach first, but she noticed that he made no attempt to assist her. When she had seated herself, he climbed in beside her and lay back with what appeared to be a sigh of relief.

"I wonder how long Eustace and his men will wait for you?" Druscilla questioned.

"I am not prepared to speculate on any of Eustace's movements," the Marquis replied in a crushing tone. "If he continues to make such a cursed nuisance of himself, I will have to deal with him, that is obvious."

"How will you do that?" Druscilla enquired.

By now the coach was driving out of the yard.

The Marquis lowered himself in his seat, stretched out his legs and put his feet on the seat opposite.

Then he tipped his hat over his eyes and said with a yawn,

"I daresay I shall contrive a way. At the moment I am too fatigued to contemplate anything except the boredom of the Ceremony that lies ahead of us."

He yawned again and Druscilla saw him close his eyes. It was obvious that he did not intend to talk to her and she felt sure that his desire to sleep was no pretence.

She turned her head to look out of the window and yet she was acutely conscious of the man beside her.

Last night he had held her in his arms. She could remember the hard strength of his mouth, the way that he crushed her to him, his kisses that seemed to sear their way into her soul and she could still feel the insistence of his lips against her neck,

She felt herself tremble, but it was not with fear.

She found herself reliving that moment when she had torn herself free of him and always she ended by hearing the anger and cynicism in the Marquis's voice.

He had hated her at that moment, hated her and despised her and she found herself longing, as she had never longed for anything before, for him to smile at her again as he had smiled at her when they were driving from the Church to Carlton House.

Why, why had she been such a fool? Why had she let her jealousy of the Duchess spoil what should have been a wonderful Wedding Day?

The Marquis had married her because he could not otherwise escape the consequences of his own lies. But had he not grown to like her a little for herself?

She amused him and he was proud of her she felt sure. Could not that have been a foundation to build their marriage on had she not spoilt everything?

Fool! *Fool!* Again she heard the wheels repeating the accusing words over and over again as they travelled over the roads. Fool! Fool!

But, when they drove down the long oak-bordered drive, she forgot everything except the joy of seeing again the house that had meant so much to her in her childhood.

It was looking more beautiful than ever. The sunshine was shining on its small-paned windows, the greystone seemed to glow like a pearl against flower-filled gardens, the lake mirrored its magnificence, the pigeons and the white doves flying across the gardens were as exquisite as she had always remembered them.

They had passed one ceremonial arch before she was aware of the Marquis at her side.

"Valdo," she said urgently, "wake up, we are there, we are at Lynche Hall!"

He opened his eyes so swiftly that she wondered if indeed he had been asleep or was merely pretending. But now she felt that his face seemed a little less drawn and the lines under his eyes not so pronounced.

"Yes, we are here," he said. "They may be surprised to see you in a riding habit, but it does not signify."

"Do I look all right?" Druscilla asked.

It was a deliberate question to make the Marquis look at her. But he seemed to be preoccupied in gazing out of the window and not to have heard her.

As the coach drew up with a flourish at the great porticoed front door, he said,

"They are waiting for us on the steps. I thought they would be."

It seemed to Druscilla that there was indeed a great crowd of people drawn up on the steps leading up to the house and round the door.

As they stepped from the coach, the Marquis' Agent began a long and formal address, which they had to listen to while being stared at by the assembled throng.

Although conducted in rather grandiose language, it was, Druscilla knew, a genuine expression of pleasure at the Marquis's marriage.

When the address was over, the Marquis introduced her to his Agent and then they started shaking hands with the household servants, the garden staff, the foresters, the stone-masons, the carpenters, the grooms and the saddlers.

It seemed to Druscilla as if the people she must greet would never come to an end.

But at last, when she felt that her hand was almost numb from being shaken so enthusiastically, she found herself walking into the Great Hall, which she had not seen since she was ten years old.

She found it now just as entrancing and just as awe-inspiring as ever.

How well she remembered the magnificence of the statues in the alcoves, the marble floor so polished that it almost mirrored those who walked on it and the great curved staircase with its carved newels.

She had never forgotten how breath-taking Lynche Hall had been to a small child.

And now she was to live here!

Little Druscilla Morley, who had only come to the Big House on sufferance because she was an obscure cousin and the daughter of the local Vicar.

She turned to tell the Marquis how thrilled she was to be back, but before she could speak he said in his most formal tones,

"I understand from Mr. Anstey that we are presiding at a dinner for the tenants at six o'clock. I would hope that your Ladyship can be ready by then. Your luggage has already arrived."

"Yes, of course," Druscilla replied. "Will it be a big party?"

The Marquis glanced towards his Agent.

"Nearly two hundred guests, my Lady."

Druscilla smiled.

"I call that a very big party! I must certainly look my best."

"I sure you will do so, my Lady."

The admiration in Mr. Anstey's eyes and in his voice was unmistakable. Somehow it was comforting as the Marquis turned away and walked towards the library.

Mr. Anstey followed him and somewhat forlornly Druscilla climbed the Great Staircase alone.

She wondered whether the Lynche ancestors were looking down at her with approval or disapproval, there were so many of them in their carved gilt frames. Was she the wife they would have accepted for the heir to their line, she wondered, had they had the choice?

Then she remembered that if it was not for her the Marquis might not be in residence at all.

For one thing he had been vowed to bachelorhood and for another he might well have been dead with a bullet blown through him by the expert shooting of the Duke of Windleham.

'I am here and you will have to put up with me,' Druscilla longed to say to the sombre eyes watching her progress to the top of the staircase.

Then to her delight she saw Rose waiting for her on the landing.

"Oh, my Lady, I've been worryin' as to what had happened to you," Rose exclaimed. "We expected you hours ago."

"Yes, we are late," Druscilla answered.

"It wasn't an accident, was it, my Lady?"

Druscilla shook her head.

"No, nothing untoward," she replied. "Where am I sleeping?"

"In here, my Lady," Rose said, opening a door off the landing. "The Bridal Chamber of all the Marchionesses of Lynche."

Druscilla entered the room and then stood very still.

She supposed that she must have seen the room as a child because she had often played in the house with Valdo, but if she had been in it before she had forgotten.

It was an enormous room with big bow-fronted windows set with tiny diamond panes overlooking the Rose Garden.

Against the wall was the largest four-poster bed that Druscilla had ever seen. All white and silver it had been carved in the reign of King Charles II with dozens of small angels flying helter-skelter over the high canopy and holding up entwined hearts.

The hangings and the bedspread were of white satin, hand-embroidered with roses and forget-me-nots, cupids and garlands.

On the floor there were white fur rugs and the furniture was all of silver, the soft burnished silver of the Restoration, each piece decorated with cupids supporting the Lynche coronet.

And, because it was the Bridal Chamber, the flowers were white too.

There were lilies, roses and carnations scenting the air with a fragrance that seemed to speak of love as clearly as the cupids who flew on their silver wings above the bed.

"It's lovely," Druscilla whispered, hardly breathing the words.

She walked across the room to stare out of the window. How well she knew her way around those dark woods behind the house and the hiding places in the shrubberies where she and Valdo had played together.

She could see some of the trees that they had climbed and the goldfish pond where they had caught the little fish and put them back again. She could see the nuttery where they had vied with the squirrels as to who should pick the nuts.

And far in the distance she thought that she could see a glimmer of the river that fed the lake where they had swum and boated and made dams or built bridges every holiday until she had gone away from Lynche Hall never to return until today.

"Oh, Rose, I am so glad – to be back!"

She had to tell someone of her gladness, but Rose, who was taking the cover off the great bed and patting the pillows, replied,

"You have half an hour to rest, my Lady, and then I will bring in your bath and dress you. I want them here to see you lookin' as beautiful as you looked yesterday."

"I will rest," Druscilla agreed, "I am indeed a trifle weary."

It was only as Druscilla started to take off her riding habit that Rose asked,

"Why did you change, my Lady? I thought you would be wearing the blue driving coat."

"I cannot talk about it now," Druscilla replied, "I will tell you later."

It was no use lying, she thought, or pretending that she had upset something on the coat. The servants in London would be chattering nonstop about the fact that she had returned alone on horseback to collect the Marquis.

They would know, each one of them, where she had found him and Druscilla, as before, felt humiliated that the servants would gossip about her while she was well aware that it was something that would never trouble the Marquis.

She put on her nightgown and slipped into the huge bed, but she could not sleep.

She could only lie looking at the beautiful room, at the canopy over her head and at the sunlight streaming in through the open windows.

Outside she could hear the coo of the doves, the buzz of the bees and occasionally the high shrill cry of one of the peacocks that roamed the gardens.

But in the background of her thoughts there was always the Marquis. She felt that she could never forget the anger in his eyes and the depression on his face when he had come from Bianca de Silva's bedroom to find her outside.

She could still hear the fury and astonishment in his voice,

"Druscilla, what the Devil are you doing here?"

Perhaps she should have sent up a message by the insolent maidservant to inform him that she was below. As usual she had been impetuous and had acted without thinking.

She so wished now that she had never seen that pretty face against the pillows!

"Your bath is ready, my Lady."

"I must get up," Druscilla murmured.

Quite suddenly she felt reluctant to move. She was afraid of going downstairs again, of facing the Marquis and seeing the contempt in his eyes.

She wanted just to lie there and forget – but could she ever forget even for a moment?

Wearily she dragged herself out of the bed, bathed in the soft scented water and put on almost automatically the silken clothes that Rose handed her.

Her hair was arranged in front of the silver mirror and then Rose brought a gown from the wardrobe, which was filled with dozens of lovely dresses.

It was only when she was fastened into her gown that Druscilla looked at herself in the long clear glass and saw that Rose had chosen that night a white gown of soft lace unrelieved by any colour.

The tight bodice revealed the curved maturity of her small breasts, but her shoulders were bare and the dress made her look very young and very unsophisticated.

As she stared at her reflection, Druscilla realised that Rose had chosen wisely. This was how the tenants and those whom she was to meet at dinner would expect a bride to look like.

This was not the hard, glittering sophisticated creature who had startled and dazzled the fashionable world in London. This was a young girl, young, untouched and innocent, starting life anew with the man she loved.

"The man she loved!"

As Druscilla repeated the words beneath her breath, she knew them to be the truth.

She loved the Marquis!

She had not realised it until now, but suddenly she knew. The truth seared itself through her body as though a cupid had shot an arrow into her heart.

She loved him!

That was why she had been haunted and tortured by her jealousy first of the Duchess and then of Bianca de Silva.

That was why she had torn herself from his arms last night, not because she had been afraid of his kisses, but because she had been afraid of the feelings he had aroused within her, feelings that she had never known before.

'I love him – *I love him*.'

The words seemed to be written on the mirror in front of her in letters of fire.

'I love him – *I love him*.'

She had not realised it.

How crazy she had been to think of him as if he was like the other men who had attempted to touch her.

They had nauseated her, but now she wanted to feel the warmth and strength of the Marquis's lips again, she wanted his kisses, she wanted his arms round her.

'I love him!'

She could have shouted the words aloud, but instead she turned towards Rose with a sudden sharp anxiety.

"Do I look all right? Are you certain that this dress is grand enough?"

"You look like a real bride should, my Lady," Rose replied simply.

From the velvet box on the dressing table she took the Dowager's necklace and clasped it round Druscilla's neck.

"Would you rather have one of the family's, my Lady?" she enquired.

"No, no, not too many jewels, just the necklace and my engagement ring."

There was a knock at the door and Rose went to open it. She came back a moment later with a small bouquet in her hand.

"These have been sent to you, my Lady, with the compliments of the gardeners. They thought you would like to carry them tonight."

Druscilla took the bouquet from her. There were rosebuds and camellias clasped together in a tiny bouquet that charmingly enhanced the whole picture of the gown she wore.

"It's perfect," Rose exclaimed in the tones of an artist who has completed an original creation, "nothing could be lovelier. And you look very young, my Lady."

"I feel – very young – tonight," Druscilla answered.

She turned from the mirror, conscious of the tumultuous feelings within herself, feelings of both excitement and anticipation.

In a few moments she would see the Marquis again.

She must tell him and somehow she must convey to him this new wonderful knowledge that she loved him.

Perhaps he would know instinctively, she thought, that she had changed.

Then, as she walked slowly downstairs, she felt shy – shyer than she had ever felt in her whole life for after all she was only a girl going to meet the man she loved.

The Marquis was waiting for her in the Grand Salon. It was a huge room filled with treasures that each generation of Lynches had collected and passed on to their heirs.

As she entered the room, Druscilla paused for a moment and to those standing beside the Marquis she seemed like an embodiment of spring.

Her glowing red hair, the graceful slimness of her body and the wide excitement in her eyes seemed to draw the attention of everybody save that of her husband.

As if he knew instinctively the moment of her appearance, he had turned away to open a map and was deep in a discussion with one of his guests as to a right-of-way on the North side of his property.

Mr. Anstey stepped forward to greet Druscilla and presented some of the more senior tenants who were having a glass of sherry with the Marquis before they proceeded to the Banqueting Hall.

"Dinner is served, my Lord."

The butler's stentorian voice seemed to echo around the room and at last the Marquis raised his head from the plan of the estate and came towards Druscilla.

"May I escort your Ladyship into dinner?" he asked formally.

She put her fingers on his arm and felt herself tremble because she was touching him and because he was so near. But, when she looked up into his face, he was scowling.

The other guests went ahead, Druscilla and the Marquis were last and, when they entered the great Banqueting Hall, everyone stood to receive them.

The Marquis led Druscilla to the top of the table. She stood on his right and then after Grace had been said by the Parson, who had succeeded to her father's incumbency, they were all seated.

Druscilla was glad that she had Mr. Anstey on her other side, because he could point out the most important tenants and farmers and their wives and tell her a little of the history of those whom she did not know or remind her of those who had been here when she had lived in the village.

Occasionally she glanced at the Marquis, but he was deep in conversation with the lady on his left, the wife of the oldest of the tenants, and not once did he turn his head in her direction.

Soon the wine loosened the tongues of the guests and they were chattering with sometimes a roar of good humour, which Druscilla found a far more genuine sound than the brittle chatter and laughter that she had heard the night before.

The meal was indeed a very different one.

Where the Prince had ordered exotic dishes with French names, here there was good English fare, great rounds of beef, legs of mutton, pigeons turned on the spit, boars' heads, fat capons and dozens of delectable puddings swimming in cream or covered with homemade jam, all of them very much to the liking of this evening's guests.

Finally, when it seemed to Druscilla that they had been eating for hours, the Marquis rose to his feet.

He made a short speech, but a witty one. Druscilla had not heard him speak in public before and she liked the way he stood straight and still and the friendly way that he seemed to take his audience into his confidence.

Most of all she liked the way he spoke so warmly of his homecoming, his desire to improve Lynche and to make it again what it had been in his father's time, one of the finest agricultural estates in the whole length and breadth of England.

There was enormous applause when he sat down.

"Bravo! *Bravo!*" some of his red-faced hunting Squires called out and hammered the table with their hands and stamped their feet on the floor.

Then somewhat to her own surprise, Druscilla found herself rising to her feet.

Instantly there was silence and she knew that the Marquis looked at her apprehensively.

In a voice that everyone could hear quite clearly she began,

"It is not for the bride to speak on these occasions, but there is one thing I do want to say to you. Many of you knew me when I lived here as a child and many of you knew my father and my beloved mother, who rests in your churchyard."

She paused for a moment to look round at everyone present before resuming,

"It is very wonderful for me to have returned to Lynche Hall. To me it has always been the most beautiful place in the world and the place where I first found such happiness. I have never forgotten my childhood in the village and now seeing many familiar faces and knowing I am here in this sublime house makes me feel I have really come home."

She sat down with tears in her eyes and the applause was thunderous. But she hardly heard it.

As she sat down, she turned towards the Marquis and looked up into his eyes, hoping that he would understand and hoping that he would appreciate what she was trying to say.

Just for a moment it seemed he did. Their eyes met and he looked at her for the first time that day.

It seemed to Druscilla as though something magical and exciting passed between them and then abruptly, as though he forced it upon himself, the Marquis turned his eyes from hers and said in a low voice so that only she could hear,

"An excellent theatrical performance. I congratulate you."

"But I meant it," Druscilla replied, "Valdo, I meant it."

But even as she spoke he had risen to his feet and she knew that he had not heard her.

"There will be fireworks in the garden," she heard him announce, "and you will find refreshments in the Orangery."

There was another good-humoured burst of applause at this and then Druscilla's hand was once again on the Marquis's arm and he was leading her down the room and out through the open window at the far end onto the terrace.

Even as they stepped from the Banqueting Hall followed by their guests, a great burst of golden stars shattered the quiet of the night and cascaded down over the great trees onto the lake.

It was followed by a rocket, another shower of gold and soon the whole assembled throng was staring Heavenwards.

It was then that Druscilla realised that the Marquis had left her side and was moving along the terrace talking first to this man and then to another.

She was alone.

She stood for a few more moments looking up into the sky and then realised that she was very tired.

Her lack of sleep the night before, the long ride, the emotions that she had experienced, first of fear of what

~187~

Eustace was contemplating and secondly a new found love within her heart made her feel that she could endure no more.

She walked along the terrace and found that a French window that led into one of the smaller salons was open.

'I will stay here until the fireworks are over,' Druscilla mused. 'No one will want to talk to me nor indeed will they miss me while they can watch such a display.'

She seated herself on the sofa and patted one of the silk cushions behind her back. She was conscious once again of feeling very tired and yet she knew that if the Marquis came into the room she would be able to spring to her feet and run towards him.

'When everyone has gone I will tell him,' she told herself. 'I will tell him that I made a mistake last night when I forbade him to touch me and that it was because I thought he was wearing the ring of another woman and not – because I minded – his lips on – mine.'

Her eyelids dropped and she thought of the strength of his arms. She felt a little thrill go through her and that was what she had felt last night.

How foolish, how stupid she had been to send him away, to insult him and to humiliate him in a way that no man would find it easy to forgive.

She knew now that she had loved the Marquis all her life. She had loved him when they played at Lynche Hall together and when she dreamt about him after he had gone back to school.

No wonder other men had seemed revolting and no wonder she had repelled their advances! All the time she had been waiting for the boy Valdo to return to her.

She had not realised it was love that had made her slave for him, that had made her count the days until the holidays and that had made her ecstatically happy in his company even when he teased her and called her 'Carrots'.

'I loved him then!' she told herself.

She had loved him when he came rushing into the schoolroom at The Castle to hide from the rampaging throng who were chasing him.

She had loved him too, although she had not realised it, when she had backed up his lies and married him to save him from a duel.

'I love him! *I love him*!' she told herself. 'I have loved him always, all my life.'

She knew now that she had been stupid beyond words to drive him from her. He might not love her, but at least he had liked her enough to take her in his arms, to seek her mouth and to kiss her as she had never been kissed.

He might have been behaving conventionally and he might have been doing only what was expected of him, but at least she had not been revolted by him as she had been revolted by other men.

Why, why had she not accepted what he had offered? Had she but returned his kisses and had she but let him do what he wished, he might have grown to love her.

At least now they would not be estranged and he would not be looking at her with that contempt in his eyes which made her feel that there was an insurmountable barrier between them, a barrier that with every hour that passed became increasingly hard to bridge.

'I must try to make him understand,' she murmured to herself. 'Perhaps when everyone has gone I can tell him and confess to him how stupid I have been.'

And yet she knew it would be the hardest task that she had ever done.

How could one say 'I love you' to a man who looked at one with contempt when by her own sheer stupidity she had killed the first signs of affection that he had shown for her?

He despised her!

She had heard it in his voice as he had said '*a fine theatrical performance*' and she had known it when he had led her out onto the terrace and then walked away to leave her alone.

Druscilla gave a little sob.

She felt lonely and forgotten, a bride who was of no interest to anyone, not even to her own bridegroom!

CHAPTER TEN

Druscilla was woken by Rose pulling back the curtains to let the warm sunshine into the room.

For a moment she could not think where she could be and then she saw the gilt canopy over her head and the white embroidered curtains on either side of the windows.

"Is it – morning?" she asked in astonishment.

"Indeed it is, my Lady, and I am certain sure you've had a good night's sleep, which your Ladyship greatly needed."

"How did I get to bed?" Druscilla asked. "I remember sitting downstairs in the salon on the sofa. I must have fallen asleep."

"Dead to the world you were, my Lady. His Lordship carried you upstairs, I put you to bed, and you never even stirred."

"His Lordship carried me – upstairs?" Druscilla questioned.

"Yes, indeed," Rose replied. "I doubt, even if he had tried, his Lordship could have woken you."

Druscilla closed her eyes again. She wondered what Valdo must have thought when he had found her asleep on the sofa.

She had meant to wait for him and talk to him when the guests had gone, instead of which she remembered nothing except knowing that she loved him and feeling that she must somehow make amends for what she had done the night before.

Last night it had seemed so easy to think that she could put things right, but now in the clear sunlight it seemed so much more difficult.

Besides, even if he had not worn the Duchess's ring, that was no proof that he was not still infatuated with Her Grace or indeed that, if she had submitted to his kisses, he would not find his mistress infinitely more satisfying than his wife.

Druscilla, feeling as though such thoughts were taunting her, sprang out of bed saying to Rose,

"I want to get dressed, please prepare my bath immediately."

"It's ready, my Lady," Rose answered. "I've been expectin' you to ring the bell for me these past two hours, but when there were no sign of your wakin' I took it upon myself to draw the curtains. I understand there will be guests to luncheon."

"Guests to lunch!" Druscilla exclaimed. "Then what time of day is it?"

"Half an hour before noon," Rose replied and Druscilla gave an exclamation of surprise and consternation.

"It's very late. You should have woken me hours ago, Rose. What will his Lordship think if I am as tardy as this when we come to the country?"

"His Lordship will not know," Rose replied. "He went out ridin' soon after nine of the clock and has not yet returned "

Druscilla was silent, wondering whether he had some reason for riding so early or whether he felt that he must escape from the house and perhaps from her.

She dressed quickly and, arrayed in a crisp white muslin that was somehow infinitely more becoming than her sophisticated London gowns, she ran downstairs.

"You look like spring itself," a grave voice said as she thrust open the door of the salon to find Sir Anthony Headley standing at the open window, a glass of madeira in his hand.

"Anthony!" she exclaimed. "I heard that there were guests for luncheon, but I did not expect to see you."

"Valdo did not tell you?" Sir Anthony enquired.

"Tell me what?" Druscilla asked.

"That he had invited me today," Sir Anthony replied. "No, 'invited' is not the right word, *insisted* on my coming. I can assure you, Druscilla, it's dashed embarrassing for a man to play gooseberry to his best friend on his honeymoon."

"So Valdo insisted," Druscilla commented in a low voice.

She walked across the room to stare pensively into the empty grate. Sir Anthony put down his glass and came to stand beside her.

"What has gone wrong, Druscilla?" he asked.

She raised her eyes to his face enquiringly and, seeing the accusation in his eyes, she turned her head away.

"Why should you imagine anything – has gone wrong?"

There was silence for a moment and then Sir Anthony said quietly,

"Valdo came to me on his Wedding night."

"Came to – *you*?" Druscilla could hardly breathe the words.

"Yes, indeed."

"Why? What – did he say? What did – he tell you?"

The questions tumbled out of her mouth without coherent thought and Sir Anthony took both her hands in his.

"Listen, Druscilla. You may have been right the other night when you told me that I did not love you as you should be loved. But I have for both you and Valdo a deep affection and I would wish you to be happy together were it possible. Druscilla, whatever you did to Valdo the other night was cruel and, I am convinced, unnecessary."

"He did not relate to you what – happened?" Druscilla asked in a low voice.

Sir Anthony shook his head.

"He told me nothing, but I sensed that you had struck at his pride, that you had in some manner killed the hopes of happiness that I have seen so clearly rising in him this past week. I think for the first time in his life, Druscilla, Valdo believed that he had the chance of being happy, but for some unknown reason you destroyed it."

Druscilla snatched her hands away from Sir Anthony's.

"How do you know? You are – guessing."

"I am guessing correctly," Sir Anthony asserted and she felt as though he sat in judgment on her.

She did not speak and after a moment he went on,

"How could you do this to Valdo? He has suffered so intensely in the past and he has been made so utterly miserable. I could not believe it possible that you of all people could have killed his new-found confidence, the first opportunity he has had since that woman's death of finding himself again."

"I don't know – what you mean," Druscilla declared. "I swear to you, Anthony, I have no idea what you are – talking about."

"Has nobody told you what Valdo went through in his boyhood?" Sir Anthony asked. "Surely you must have heard?"

"Nobody has told me anything. I suppose I knew that he did not get on with the Marchioness, if it is she you are speaking about."

"Of course it is his stepmother I am referring to," Sir Anthony said sharply. "Did you not know how she made Valdo's life a hell after she married his father and how apart from what he himself suffered, he saw his father, the old Marquis, for whom he had a deep affection, crumbling before his very eyes under the cruelty of a woman who had married merely for what money she could extort from a sick man?"

"I did not know – that," Druscilla murmured, her voice hardly above a whisper. "I knew that her Ladyship quarrelled with a great many people – including my father. That is why we left the village."

"She was a fiend incarnate," Sir Anthony went on. "I used to come home with Valdo in the vacations from Oxford University because he begged me to do so. He could not face her alone. I saw the way that she taunted him and the way that she browbeat, deceived and insulted her husband. I saw the servants cringe before her."

He coughed and then continued,

"I think, if the truth be known, she was a trifle mad, but that was no consolation to those who were subjected to her tyrannical rages, her lies, her deceits and the way that she would find the weak spot in a man and jeer and sneer at him until he felt that she was twisting a dagger in an open wound."

"Why did Valdo endure it?" Druscilla asked.

"He loved his father," Sir Anthony replied simply. "He would put up with anything to help the Marquis. He knew how much his presence counted to a man who was slowly dying. But it left its mark, can you not understand that?"

"It made him swear that he would never get married?" Druscilla said in a low voice.

"Exactly. He mistrusted all women. After his mother died he had never found tenderness, gentleness or understanding in his own home, only hatred and cruelty. That was why he swore to me and to all his friends that he would never expose himself to such suffering as his father had suffered."

Druscilla put her hands up to her face.

She could see it all too clearly, the young, gay laughing Valdo whom she had known as a child turned into a disillusioned and cynical man.

"But," she said aloud, "he has had many – loves."

"Why not?" Sir Anthony asked almost roughly. "Valdo has been pursued by women for his looks, his wealth and for himself ever since I can remember. Never once has he asked one to be his wife until he met you."

Druscilla turned and walked towards the window. How could she explain that it had not been intentional on Valdo's part and that it had just been the force of circumstances?

"When I saw you," Sir Anthony went on, "I understood why."

Druscilla longed to scream out at him that he did not understand at all and that it was all very different from what he imagined.

Valdo was no starry-eyed lover laying his heart at the feet of a young girl who had woken within him the love that he thought he would never find.

It was not that the citadel which he had built round himself had crumbled at her appearance, but rather that she had been forced upon him because there was no alternative.

"You don't – understand," she murmured weakly.

He came close to her.

"What do I not understand?" he asked. "When Valdo came to me on his Wedding night bedevilled and mad as fire about something that you had done to him, it would have given me the greatest pleasure to take a whip to you."

She glanced up in surprise and startled at the anger in his voice.

"I mean that," he went on grimly. "No one knows better than I what Valdo is like in reality. Beneath the social figure and beneath all the trappings of his coronet and his wealth is a man, Druscilla, a man that other men respect. I have fought beside Valdo in battle, I have shared hunger and even on one occasion defeat with him and all I can tell you is that I admire him more than any other man I have ever met in my whole life."

There was a silence for a moment and then Sir Anthony continued,

"And yet a girl, a woman who I thought was different from the ordinary bird-brained Society chit, could send him to me blue about the gills with a look in his eyes that I have not seen since we carried in our dead after a battle and found that they had been mutilated by the enemy."

Druscilla gave a little cry and put her hands up to her ears.

"Stop, *stop*!" she pleaded. "You don't understand what you are saying. It was not my fault – it was not what you think."

"I don't know what I do think," Sir Anthony replied. "It is only Valdo I am concerned with and, as we sat drinking all through the night together, I became more and more determined that I should tell you the truth and that you should realise that by some cork-brained stupidity you are destroying something precious and fine and you will regret it for the rest of your whole life."

"Valdo was with you all – night?" Druscilla questioned him in a low voice.

"All night and about dawn he fell asleep on my bed and I let him rest."

Druscilla stared at him incredulously unable to speak.

"He was extremely foxed by that time," Sir Anthony said with a twist of his lips, "that was why I sent a note to tell you to get ahead. I thought it was best for you not to see the effect that your Wedding night had had on your bridegroom."

Druscilla drew in a deep breath.

"But he went from you to – Bianca de Silva."

Sir Anthony looked startled.

"How do you know that?" he enquired. "Valdo must be deranged if he tells you things like that."

"He did not – tell me," Druscilla answered hesitatingly, "I-I found out."

"There are things that a refined female should have no knowledge about," Sir Anthony said sternly. "But if you want the truth, Valdo told me when he left my lodgings that he was going to pay Miss de Silva off. He had forgotten about her in all the excitement over the Wedding and she had sent him a note complaining of his treatment. So he said that on his way back to Lynche Hall he would stop at her flat in Half Moon Street and give her the go-by."

The Marquis had been paying off his mistress!

Somehow the sunshine seemed more golden than it was before. Druscilla clasped her hands together and a sudden feeling of irrepressible joy rose within her breast.

So she had been wrong – wrong about the Duchess and wrong about Bianca de Silva.

How could she have been so foolish? And yet everything had conspired to deceive her, the rings that looked alike and the fact that she had found her husband in his mistress's bedroom.

For the first time that vision of a lovely pouting face and the fair hair spread over the pillows faded and also for the first time since her marriage the Duchess no longer seemed a menace.

Impulsively she turned towards Sir Anthony.

"Thank you for telling me all this," she said softly.

"But it could not have been that unimportant bit of muslin that you quarrelled about," he declared.

"No, it was not about Bianca de Silva."

"Someone else?" Sir Anthony enquired. "Ever since your engagement to Valdo has been announced there has been no one else, Druscilla, I know, because I have been with him nearly all the time and he has thought of no one else except you. There have been no notes, no assignations, no clandestine meetings and no shred of interest in the lovebirds who he once spent so much of his time with."

Sir Anthony sighed before he went on,

"I began to think that at last he had found what he has been looking for all his life, someone to love and someone who would love him."

He paused before he continued slowly as if he chose every word with care,

"Then Valdo came to me on his Wedding night, his eyes dark, the cynical lines back on his face, the misery and darkness that had encompassed him during his youth clinging round him like an impenetrable fog. How could you, Druscilla, how could you do anything so heartless?"

"I cannot – explain," Druscilla answered brokenly, "but I will try to – put things right, I will – really."

Sir Anthony smiled at her and held out his hands.

"Promise me that. Oh, Druscilla, you are so lovely, and I am sure that you could make Valdo or any other man happy if you wished to do so. Surely it is not difficult for two people, each in their own way so attractive, so absurdly good-looking and so blessed with everything that is important in life to find happiness together.

"I think first," Druscilla said in a very low voice, "they have to find – love."

"Then find it," Sir Anthony urged, "find it quickly before you lose Valdo. You can drive a man too far, Druscilla, and, if you spoil his happiness as it has been spoilt before by his stepmother, then there is no knowing what will happen."

"I will not spoil it – *I will not*," Druscilla said in a sudden panic. "Oh, Anthony, help me – help me."

"You know I will, Druscilla," Sir Anthony answered. "I love you both."

His eyes were very tender as he rested them on her little face and saw the anxiety in her eyes.

Then there was the sound of footsteps crossing the hall, the door opened and they drew apart.

The Marquis came in still wearing his riding clothes and accompanied by two local Squires whom he had invited to lunch. Druscilla knew that they were his defence against having to talk to her.

He bowed to her formally.

"Good morning, Druscilla," he said in an impersonal tone that he might easily have addressed a stranger in. "I trust your Ladyship slept well."

"I am afraid I was – very tired," Druscilla replied. "It must have been inconvenient for you – to carry me to bed."

Quite suddenly she felt shy. There was something embarrassing in the thought that he had held her close in his arms and taken her up the Grand Staircase and laid her down on her bed.

What had he thought, she wondered, as he looked at her sleeping face, her eyelashes dark against her cheeks?

Had he wanted to kiss the lips which were still a little bruised from his strength the night before or had he felt merely revulsion because of the way that she had treated him?

It was difficult to know what he did think. The Marquis was talking quite naturally with his friends, laughing over affairs of the estate, greeting Sir Anthony with a warmth that gave Druscilla a pang of jealousy because of the difference from the cold voice that he had spoken to her in.

They went into luncheon and she took her place at the opposite end of the table to the Marquis. Since therefore they were separated by the gold ornaments, the hothouse flowers and great bowls of grapes and peaches, there was no necessity for him to include her in his conversation.

He talked to the man on his right and on his left and she was left to converse with Sir Anthony, who she knew was watching her with critical eyes.

She found that she was not hungry and sent away dish after dish untouched.

Although she tried to concentrate on what Sir Anthony was saying, she found herself instead listening to the Marquis, noting every intonation in his voice and wondering if he was as tinglingly aware of her as she was of him.

It seemed to Druscilla that the meal was endless.

Finally they rose from the table and then the Marquis immediately suggested that the gentlemen should repair to the stables where he had some new horses in training.

He did not include Druscilla in the invitation and, making no effort to thrust herself forward, she could only watch them a little wistfully as they walked away down the wide steps outside the front door.

She heard their laughter long after they were out of sight.

As soon as she was alone, all Sir Anthony's revelations and reproaches flooded back into her mind.

How could she have known, she asked herself, but she could find no good excuse for not having tried to discover really why the Marquis had sworn to remain a bachelor.

Only a stupid and insensitive person would have behaved as she had in not questioning the Dowager more closely and trying to understand his motives.

She saw how selfish she had been in thinking only of herself and of her own sufferings.

She had forgotten that other people could be unhappy too and other people could be tortured just as she had been in different circumstances.

If Lynche Hall meant so much to her, she thought, how much more must it mean to the Marquis. It had been his home ever since he had been born.

He was part of it because it had been handed down to him by generation after generation of his own blood.

'I have been insensitive and exceedingly foolish,' Druscilla told herself and suddenly she knew what she must do.

Slipping upstairs to her room she took a bonnet from the cupboard without sending for Rose and set it on her head.

Then without even glancing at herself in the mirror she ran downstairs and set off to walk across the Park to the little greystone Church.

It was quite a long walk, but her pace was hurried and her cheeks were warm when finally she turned in at the small lychgate and saw the overgrown churchyard with its crooked tombstones just the same as it had been when she had left the village nine years before.

She opened the Church door and knew that she would have recognised the smell of damp, mildew and fading flowers anywhere in the world.

There was a feeling of age and changelessness and an atmosphere of faith, the simple uncomplicated faith of those who lived in the county and to whom Nature was very near to God.

Druscilla walked up the aisle and knelt in the pew where she had sat Sunday after Sunday with her mother.

She almost expected to look up into the pulpit and see her father droning away on some long theological discourse that was far above the heads of his simple congregation.

Then she knew that it was not here that she wanted to pray but outside in the sunshine by the grave that held her mother – a simple grave surmounted only by a plain granite cross that stood in the shady corner by an ancient yew tree.

She went there, falling on her knees in the long uncut grass and looking through eyes suddenly blurred with tears at her mother's name – Harriet Mary Morley.

They were just words on a stone, but Druscilla felt that somewhere her mother was waiting for her, listening for her, striving to help her and holding out her arms to her as she had done so often when she was a child.

'Oh, Mama, Mama,' Druscilla prayed, 'Help me now! I have made such a coil of everything and I love him. I did not realise it before – but I have always loved him. Make him understand, make him love me, if only a little, so that we can be – happy together.'

It was a prayer that came from the very depths of Druscilla's whole being and as she bowed her head she felt as though her mother was near her. She felt too as if all the defiance as well as the terror that she had lived with for so long were wiped away.

She was no longer battling against the world and especially against men, she was just the simple-hearted trusting girl she had been when her mother was alive.

How kind everyone had been and how understanding and, because she had received kindness, she had given it. It was only when she found herself alone that terror and hatred had twisted her whole outlook on life, making everything ugly and frightening.

'Teach me to think of other people rather than myself, Mama,' she prayed, 'and especially Valdo – I love him – I love him with all my heart.'

She must have knelt for a long time, striving to reach her mother and striving to make her prayer a very real one.

Then she was conscious with a vivid awareness of the birds singing in the trees, of the fragrance of newly mown hay and of the sunshine warm upon her bare arms.

She rose to her feet and knew that she was comforted and that she was now at peace.

It was a peace that she had not known for many years and not since her mother had died had she felt so at one with the world or so in tune with all creation.

Slowly she walked back through the Park and now there was no hurry.

She knew what she had to do and, although it would be hard, she felt that her mother would help her to find the right way and the right approach.

'I love Valdo – I will make him happy.'

The words were a vow. She would love him, help him, comfort him and make him realise that not all women were like the one who had destroyed his happiness in his boyhood.

Almost as though she heard her mother speak, she knew that the only way to make Valdo love her was to give him all her love, her whole heart and her whole soul.

She had not realised this before, she had held back, suspicious and untrusting because of what she herself had suffered.

But now she knew that all thoughts of self must be put aside, it was only love that could bring her love and only through love could she make him understand.

For the rest of the afternoon she was alone, but she was not lonely. The Marquis and Sir Anthony returned shortly before dinner, but she did not see them until she came downstairs to the salon.

She had taken a great deal of trouble over her appearance and she hoped that the Marquis would notice.

The dress she was wearing, of deep blue tulle spangled with tiny stars, made her skin look dazzlingly white. Her hair, arranged in a new fashion, was like tongues of flame curling over her head.

She had anticipated that they would be alone, just the three of them, but to her disappointment she found that the Marquis had invited the Agent and his wife to dinner and also a middle-aged man who was staying with them.

They were nice people and Druscilla liked them, but she found it hard to concentrate on what they were saying and difficult to listen to anything but the Marquis's voice and almost impossible to look at anyone except at her husband.

Once again it seemed to her that the Marquis did not even glance in her direction and that his voice when he spoke to her was icily cold. She felt her spirits sink lower and lower as the evening wore on.

The men played whist after dinner and Druscilla made polite conversation with the Agent's wife.

She was absorbed only in her children and the works on the estate and, although Druscilla tried hard to seem interested, she was glad when the guests said that they must return home and she could say 'goodbye' to them.

She hoped that there would be a chance to talk to the Marquis and she knew that she had only to signal to Sir Anthony that she wished to be alone and he would leave them.

The Marquis, however, circumvented her.

"It's about time we had a session at piquet, Anthony," he said. "I feel like gambling tonight and, as you have a deuce of a lot of my soft put away, I demand my revenge. Come along I will bid you a monkey for each hand."

"I should be in my cups to accept such stakes as well you know," Sir Anthony replied. "Besides I am not certain that I wish to play piquet at this time of night."

"This time of night!" the Marquis roared. "Why, it's not yet eleven o'clock. You are not going to fob me off with that sort of excuse!"

The Marquis seated himself firmly at the card table that had been laid out at one end of the salon and Druscilla realised that it would be hopeless for her to try to speak to him at this moment.

"If you are determined to spend the night gambling," she said, "I had best retire to bed. Goodnight, Anthony, goodnight – Valdo."

Her voice lingered on his name as he rose to his feet and bowed.

"Goodnight, Druscilla."

He did not look at her and with a feeling of despair she went from the room and up the stairs.

She did not go to bed.

When Rose had undressed her, she sat at the window gazing out at the night.

It was two hours later before she heard the Marquis and Sir Anthony come upstairs. Just for a moment she contemplated going to her husband's room, which was only just across the passage from hers.

But she knew that she could not face the hard look of enquiry in his eyes were she to do so. That, she was sure, was not the way to approach him. He would not understand.

But how, how could she ever see him when he was so determined that they should not be alone together?

Sooner or later there must be an opportunity, but she knew how difficult it was going to be.

Almost without her realising it, tears sprang from her eyes and ran down her cheeks.

It was a long time later that she noticed a strange smell. At first she could not think what it was and then she realised that it came not from the garden but from the house.

She rose from the window seat feeling how cramped she had become sitting there for so long and aware too that, although the night was warm, she was chilled.

She shivered a little as she crossed the room.

Now she could smell it even stronger.

There was no mistaking it – it was smoke.

She opened her door and looked out into the passage.

Although the tapers had been extinguished in the sconces, the moonlight shining through the great diamond-paned windows that ran the whole length of one side of the hall gave enough light for her to see that the corridor was empty.

At the same time the smell of smoke was almost overpowering.

Then something flickered red as fire.

She ran across the landing and, looking down over the staircase, saw with a sense of shock a figure with a lighted torch applying it to one of the silk curtains that hung on either side of the windows.

One was already ablaze and as she watched the other one was set aflame, the fire running fiercely up the silk.

Druscilla wanted to scream, but her voice died in her throat as she recognised the man who held the torch, recognised him by the shape of his head and the low insane chuckle he gave as he turned with his torch towards yet another curtain.

For a moment Druscilla stood there paralysed and then she turned in terror and thrust open the door of the Marquis's bedroom.

There were two candles alight. She looked first towards the bed to find it empty and then she saw him seated half-dressed in the high wing-chair beside the hearth.

He had taken off his coat and cravat, but was still wearing his frilled white shirt, which was now open at the neck, and the skin-tight yellow pantaloons that he had worn for dinner.

His feet were thrust out in front of him, his head was against the back of the chair and he was asleep.

Druscilla ran towards him.

"Valdo, *Valdo!*" she cried and, as he did not wake, she put her hands on his shoulders and shook him. "Valdo, wake up!"

He woke up with a start to stare at her almost incredulously. Her face was close to his and her hair was shining in the light of the candles.

"It's Eustace! Eustace! He is here, downstairs, setting the house on fire!"

"*Eustace!*"

The Marquis cried out the name like a pistol shot and sprang to his feet. He moved towards the door, but, as he did so, Druscilla put out her hand instinctively.

"Be careful, for God's sake, Valdo, be very careful. He is dangerous."

"It is I who will be dangerous, curse him if he thinks he can burn down my house," the Marquis asserted in a tone of fury. "Rouse the servants!"

Then he was gone.

Druscilla was still for a moment and then back from the past came the memory of being shown as a little girl the fire bells that stood on every floor of the house.

She remembered how she had longed to pull the thick long ropes, but Valdo had warned her that if she did so without due cause she would never be allowed to come to the house again.

"It will bring out everybody," he told her, "servants, gardeners, estate workers. They all come when they hear the bell."

In a kind of panic she thought that first she had forgotten where the bell was and then she remembered. It was in the passage just beyond the first landing.

It was opposite his Lordship's bedroom, she had been told, and she recalled where Valdo's father had slept.

She ran towards it. It meant passing across the hall and when she did she saw that the fire had gained a good hold on the curtains and the flames were flaring high.

She looked for Eustace, but he was no longer there nor was there any sign of the Marquis.

Then suddenly she heard someone laugh and looking up she saw them both running up the stairs towards the second floor with Eustace waving his fiery torch, its sparks flying off in every direction.

Behind him, half a flight away, was the Marquis.

"Stop, Eustace, stop, *damn you!*" he shouted, but in reply there was only the sound of Eustace's mad laughter.

'He is crazy, completely crazy,' Druscilla thought and she ran on and found the fire bell where she had remembered it would be.

She tugged at the rope and for a moment she thought that she was too weak to pull it or else it had rusted from disuse.

But at last it began to ring with a loud clanging that seemed almost deafening in the empty dark night.

She went on pulling and pulling almost wildly and all the time she realised that the smoke from the hall was getting denser and she was beginning to find it difficult to breathe.

Then at last there was the sound of voices and people were running from every direction.

After a long time someone lifted her up in his arms and she realised that it was Sir Anthony.

"The bell – the bell!" she managed to stammer to him.

"It's all right, they are all warned," he answered. "Put your face against my shoulder. I have to get you out of this."

He carried her along the passage and down under another staircase. This was also full of smoke, but it was not as thick as that coming from the hall.

"The salon is alight," she heard someone shout.

There was the shrill scream of a young maid and a sudden crash as though something was overturned.

Then she felt the fresh air on her face and raised her eyes from Sir Anthony's shoulder to find that they were outside.

There seemed to be a lot of people assembled already in the courtyard outside the front door and even as Druscilla looked round there was the crunch of wheels and the estate fire engine drawn by eight men came from the direction of the stables.

And now someone, she thought that it was the Major Domo, was organising a chain of buckets from the lake and the estate firemen were unwinding the hoses.

She wondered if anything would be effective against the flames leaping against the diamond-paned windows.

From this side of the house she could only see the flames in the hall, but she could hear men shouting that water was required on the other side to save the salon.

Pictures and furniture were being carried out by men who were coughing as they emerged from the smoke.

Druscilla had only one thought – Valdo.

Where was he and where had he gone in pursuit of Eustace? She stared at the upper windows of the house, but they were all dark.

"Valdo – he is in – danger!" she managed to blurt out and Sir Anthony looked down at her in surprise.

"In danger?" he asked. "From the fire?"

"No, no, from Eustace! It was he who set the house on fire."

"Eustace! I might have guessed it," Sir Anthony said in tones of disgust.

"They were both running upstairs before I rang the bell," Druscilla exclaimed.

Sir Anthony turned his head upwards and even as he did so there came a gasp from the crowd.

Two men had appeared on the roof. It was easy to see them in the moonlight.

Valdo, very conspicuous in his white shirt, was pursuing the more soberly clad figure of Eustace, who was leaping wildly across the tiles and Druscilla could almost fancy that she could hear his mad laughter.

Then suddenly they came to the parapet and while Druscilla looked, quite bereft of speech, she saw Eustace climb onto the narrow greystone that surrounded the house, holding onto one of the ornamental urns that it was graced with.

Something glinted in the moonlight and she saw that in his hand he held a long stiletto-like dagger, which she knew without being told he must have taken from the wall of the armoury as he had run through it.

There was a large amount of warlike weapons there collected over the years and amongst them would have been this sharp steel dagger, the point of which could enter a man's heart and kill him.

Druscilla clutched at Sir Anthony's arm in sudden terror. She felt that he was equally tense, but there was nothing they could do.

They could only stand below and watch the two men high above them facing each other.

Now the Marquis, weaponless and an easy target in his white shirt, was moving towards his cousin.

It was impossible to hear what he said, but Druscilla knew that he was ordering Eustace, or perhaps coaxing him, to throw down the weapon he held in his hand.

But, as the Marquis moved nearer still to him, they saw Eustace draw back his arm, the dagger flashing as he did so.

Then he threw it, throwing it fiercely with an almost diabolical strength straight at the man approaching him.

The Marquis staggered and Druscilla gave a little cry.

But, as he struck at his cousin, Eustace had relinquished his hold on the urn and in doing so lost his balance.

There was just one moment when he seemed to hover weaponless between earth and sky before with a shrill shriek that could be heard high above the noise of the fire and the voices of those fighting it, he fell.

Even as he did so, Druscilla saw the Marquis fall too and heard her own voice, strangely unreal, cry out,

"He has killed him – *oh, God, he has killed – Valdo*!"

CHAPTER ELEVEN

The Marquis was suddenly aware of voices deliberately kept low and soft, the voices of two people talking very near him.

Unable at first to understand where he was and what had happened, he heard the voice of his valet saying,

"I pray your Ladyship to let me sit up with his Lordship tonight. You've been with him for four nights now and at his bedside all through the days as well. 'Tis too much for your Ladyship. Get an hour or so of sleep, I swear I'll wake you if there be any change."

"No, Jenkins, you have had as much to do as I have," the Marquis heard Druscilla say in a gentle rather tired voice. "His Lordship was not as restless last night as he was the night before. I feel sure he is definitely getting better."

"That is what the doctor says, my Lady, and he says too it's real gratifyin' how quick the wound in his Lordship's shoulder has healed."

"It was not the wound we were most worried about," Druscilla said with a little sigh, "it was that terrible bruise on his head where he fell against the parapet. The doctor says it's a miracle he did not crack his skull."

"Now, my Lady, don't you worry yourself! His Lordship's very tough, he'll soon be a-toolin' his horses again."

"I am sure he will be, Jenkins. It's just that I have not yet got over that first shock when I thought that Mr. Eustace had killed him."

"The whole thing was too much of a shock if you ask me, my Lady, what with the house on fire, Mr. Eustace lyin' dead on the gravel and his Lordship more like a corpse than a livin' man. It be a wonder all our very hairs didn't turn as white as Christmas."

Druscilla gave a little gurgle of laughter.

"Oh, Jenkins, you are so funny the way you say it, but it's true enough. And yet it is amazing how little damage the fire did after all. New curtains will be required in the hall, several carpets must be repaired and the salon will have to be redecorated. To tell the truth I am not altogether sorry about that. I did not like that ugly mustard colour that the late Marchioness had chosen. I am delighted it is to be replaced."

"Well, my Lady, you'll be a-talkin' it over with his Lordship in a few days, you mark my words."

"Will – I?" Druscilla asked almost beneath her breath.

The Marquis felt, although he did not open his eyes, that she had moved a little nearer and was standing at the bedside looking down at him.

"He looks so weak and so helpless," she murmured as if she spoke to herself.

"Now, my Lady, don't you go upsettin' yourself again," Jenkins admonished her. "You've been through enough. I've said already it's too much for you a-sittin' up night after night, though it be true that your Ladyship was the only one who could manage to soothe his Lordship when he was so restless, throwin' himself about and cryin' out. I often wondered who it was he was a-callin' for?"

"I too have been wondering that," Druscilla admitted. "It was somebody he wanted very much – somebody who mattered a great deal to him."

There was silence and then Jenkins said hastily,

"Is there anythin' else you want, my Lady? Some fresh lemonade? There's a warm kettle on the hearth. Your Ladyship knows that, if you need me, you have only to touch the bell. It rings in my room and I'll be down here within a few seconds."

"Yes, I know you will and thank you, Jenkins, you have been a tower of strength these past few days. I don't know how I could have managed without you."

"If you would only listen to me and have a good night's sleep, my Lady – " Jenkins began only to be interrupted by Druscilla.

"No, we cannot go through all that again. I will look after his Lordship until he regains consciousness. Then it will be – your turn, Jenkins. And don't forget your promise – that you will never let him know that I have nursed him."

"I've given you my word, my Lady, though it goes against the grain to lie to his Lordship, especially as it looks like he owes his life to your Ladyship's care of him."

"You promised, Jenkins."

"Very well, my Lady. Don't hesitate to ring if you're in need of me."

"I will not. Goodnight, Jenkins, and thank you."

The Marquis heard the door close.

He lay very still in the bed.

Now he could remember seeing Eustace standing on the parapet, the dagger raised in his hand. Then he saw it coming at him. He had tried to turn aside, but felt a sharp pain in his shoulder and because he was turning he was caught off-balance.

He remembered struggling to save himself and then there had been darkness, nothing but darkness.

As well he seemed to recall that he had called out, seeking for someone.

Now he knew that it had just been a figment of his imagination, a strange unaccountable dream when he had been looking, searching and striving to find someone who eluded him. He felt very weak.

At the same time his brain was clear and he knew without opening his eyes that Druscilla had not sat down in the chair but was still standing beside his bed.

Suddenly she came nearer. He felt her kneel down beside him and something silky fell against his face.

He smelt a sweet fragrance that reminded him of spring flowers.

"Oh, my darling," he heard her say very softly, "if only I could give you – some of my strength."

Then he felt the touch of her lips warm and yet soft as a butterfly's wing on his cheek.

*

The sunshine was reflected iridescently golden in the mirror that Druscilla stared into with unseeing eyes.

Rose was doing her hair, looping it carefully and fastening the curls down with hairpins because later she was going to go riding.

"Shall I fetch your habit now, my Lady?" she asked when she had finished.

Druscilla gave a start because she had hardly been aware of what was happening.

"No, not yet, Rose," she answered after a moment's pause. "It's very hot and I have some letters to write. I will not dress yet. Give me a wrapper to wear over my nightgown and I will ring in about an hour's time."

"Very good, my Lady."

Rose brought Druscilla a lace-trimmed chiffon wrapper from the wardrobe.

Druscilla slipped her arms into the wide sleeves and the wrapper floating around her was like the mist above the lake. It did little to hide the exquisite lines of her slim nakedness.

Then, moving noiselessly in her heelless white satin slippers, she walked from the bedroom into the boudoir adjoining it.

Here the room was fragrant with the scent of flowers and the sunshine was coming through the lattice-paned windows to throw strange patterns on the carpet.

The carpet was woven with flying cupids bearing blue ribbons towards great clusters of roses and just as in the

~215~

bedroom there were cupids carved on the mirrors and on the furniture.

There were even cupids on the ormolu ink-stand that Druscilla dipped a large white quill into as she drew some writing paper towards her.

She was still writing letters of thanks for the gifts that she and the Marquis had received on their Wedding Day.

But she had been sadly behind in her work during the last week when she had watched hour after hour beside his bedside and had only left him when she was so desperately tired that she had to snatch a few hours sleep before continuing her vigil.

Now he was better she had left his bedchamber one morning early to bathe and change her clothes when Jenkins had come running in excitedly to tell her that his Lordship was awake, sensible in all he was saying and asking for food.

"Give it to him, Jenkins, give his Lordship everything he wants."

"Won't you come and see him yourself, my Lady?" Jenkins asked.

Druscilla shook her head.

"Not unless he asks for me, Jenkins, and then, of course, I will come at once."

She had waited all that day and all the next, but the Marquis had not asked for her. She had known then that he did not intend to do so.

Jenkins brought her almost hourly bulletins of the Marquis's progress.

The doctor was pleased with him. He was tired, still subject to headaches, but he was eating well and was determined to recover his strength as quickly as possible.

It seemed to Druscilla as though an invisible barrier still stood between them.

It was only a few steps from her room to that occupied by the Marquis and yet as far as she was concerned they might be hundreds of miles apart.

She hoped almost against hope that there might be some valid excuse for her to ask to see him or that he would wish to consult her about the damage done to the house by the fire.

But the days passed and she sensed that Jenkins was embarrassed by the fact that the Marquis never mentioned her name.

The valet had no idea how greatly she longed for news of her husband or that sometimes when everyone was asleep she would stand in the corridor outside his bedroom listening.

She was hoping, although she knew that it was wrong of her, that she would hear his voice ranting again in delirium.

Then she would have an excuse to go to him, to put her hand on his brow to soothe him and even to hold his head against her breasts as she had done those first nights after the accident when no one else could keep him quiet and when he would respond to no one but her.

*

It was very quiet at Lynche Hall.

Sir Anthony had gone back to London, Eustace's body had been removed to his own home in Hertfordshire where he was to be buried and the servants, as was to be expected in the case of illness, moved unobtrusively about the house.

Druscilla felt herself isolated almost as though she was living on another planet. She would know nothing, hear nothing and be nothing until the Marquis was well again.

She would lie awake night after night in the great bridal bed trying to find words in which to reveal to him how foolish she had been on their Wedding night.

She wanted to explain the mistake that she had made over the rings, she wanted to tell him too how deeply she had suffered, although she had hardly realised it at the time, when she had learnt that he had a mistress.

How birdbrained she had been to let these things trouble her and yet she knew that they were but natural jealousy because she had loved him almost without knowing it.

He had always been there in her heart, the man she had been seeking all her life, transformed from the boy she had loved into a man she loved without realising it – until it was too late.

Now she realised how hard and defiant she had grown these past years simply because of what she had suffered at the hands of other men.

She had been on the defensive with her repulsion and terror making her anticipate attacks from every side.

She had not only been afraid of men, she had been afraid of love and like an animal who has been cruelly treated, she was ready to bite the hand even of someone who was trying to be kind to her.

At this moment she had lost not only her defiance but also her defences. She felt helplessly weak, feminine and despondent as she cried night after night into her pillow because of the hopelessness of it all.

She was all woman, a woman who loved a man with her heart and her whole being and could think of nothing else.

Because she wanted to be loved herself, she began now to prize her beauty as much as she had hated it before.

She made Rose try new ways of arranging her hair and she tried to find blemishes on the clear perfection of her skin so that she could erase them before the Marquis could see them.

She saw how many of the gowns in her trousseau were exceedingly smart, but they seemed to her hard and flamboyant and she was determined never to wear them again.

Druscilla, unable to concentrate on the letter she was supposed to be writing, found herself gazing out of the window. Her eyes were sad and wistful and there was a little droop at the corners of her mouth.

Her thoughts were far away when there came a knock at the door.

"Come in," she called out automatically.

Feeling rather like a child who has been caught out neglecting her lessons, she picked up her pen again and looked down at the letter on which she had written but one short sentence.

"I came to bid you 'good morning'," a deep voice said from behind her.

She gave a startled cry and sprang up from the writing table to see that the Marquis stood there.

He came into the room, closing the door behind him.

He was dressed in the height of fashion and he looked exceedingly elegant and very handsome, but Druscilla saw that some of the tan had gone from his face and he was thinner than he had been before his illness.

"I was – not expecting – you," Druscilla said, conscious that her heart was beating feverishly beneath the diaphanous chiffon of her nightgown and the transparent lace trimmed wrapper.

The Marquis did not speak and she said hurriedly and stammering her embarrassment,

"Are you – b-better? You are not doing – t-too much – too quickly? You must be careful of your – shoulder."

"I am well," the Marquis replied firmly. "The doctor has been this morning and declared that there is no reason for him to make any further visits unless I should send for him."

"Oh, I am g-glad about that, so v-very glad," Druscilla murmured.

The Marquis moved along the room to stand in front of the fireplace.

She felt that she had forgotten how tall he was, how broad-shouldered and how big he seemed beside herself.

"Will you not – sit down?" she asked, her voice unsteady because of the tumult within her.

"Thank you," he replied.

He seated himself in a brocade armchair and looked across the room at her.

"I sincerely hope that you are pleased to perceive that I am now in good health."

"Of course – I am," she answered. "But it is such a – surprise! I had thought that Jenkins would tell me when you were ready – to leave your room."

"He wanted to do so, but I forbade him. I wished to show you myself that I was entirely recovered."

"I am glad," Druscilla repeated in a low voice.

"I also want to talk to you, Druscilla," he then said.

She thought that he spoke somewhat sternly and felt her heart contract with sudden fear.

"What is it?" she asked.

"I wanted to tell you," the Marquis said slowly as if he were choosing his words with care, "that I have fallen in love."

Druscilla felt as though she was turned to stone.

For a moment she could only stare at him while the blood receded from her face leaving her very pale.

Then with a strangled sound that was almost a cry she turned and walked to the window.

She stood with her hands gripping the window frame, staring out into the sunlit garden, feeling as though the whole world had fallen about her ears.

So this was why he had not asked to see her and why he had not even sent her a message.

He was in love and now he would want to be released from his marriage, this false mockery of a marriage that had been forced upon him by circumstances in which it seemed the only possible way of escape for him.

He was in love and there was no longer any room for her in his life.

She wanted to cry out at the unbearable pain within her heart.

Then pride came to the rescue.

He must never know that she loved him.

With an almost superhuman effort at self-control she said without turning her head,

"I am – grateful that you are – frank with me. What do you – wish me to – do?"

"I want your help," the Marquis responded in a deep voice.

Druscilla closed her eyes against the sunshine. She knew what he was going to ask. He would ask her to go away, he would offer her money, perhaps a great deal of money, if she would set him free.

She would be able to go anywhere, anywhere in the world, except to live at Lynche Hall, which she loved and which had become an indivisible part of herself.

But nothing – not even separation from Lynche Hall mattered beside the fact that she would never again be with Valdo, never see him or hear him or belong to him.

She hoped despairingly that she would not live long and that the agony she was suffering now would kill her.

She was still fighting for her breath, but she managed to say, although even to herself her voice sounded strange,

"How – can I – help you?"

"I have lost the woman I love," the Marquis replied.

"You have – lost her?"

Druscilla could not repress the surprise in her voice and she was so astonished that she turned round to stare at him.

He was sitting back in the armchair.

And it seemed to her that there was an expression on his face that she had never seen before.

"Yes, I have lost her," the Marquis repeated, "and I beg of you, Druscilla, to help me to find her because I know I shall never be happy until I do."

"Do you – love her so – much?" Druscilla asked and each word was so agonising that she felt that they stabbed her fatally.

"I love her with all my heart and soul. I did not realise it before. I have loved her for a long time, but I did not recognise love for what it was. I thought it was many things, physical attraction, the satisfaction of desire and the pleasure of having a woman in one's arms and of knowing that she was responding to the need one felt for her. I know now that is not love."

"Then – what is – love?" Druscilla managed to ask him.

"I think love is when a man feels that he belongs to a woman and she belongs to him," the Marquis said slowly, "when he knows that they are together as one person so that without her he is incomplete."

Druscilla remembered herself saying something almost the same to Sir Anthony.

She felt the tears come into her eyes and she turned back to the window so that the Marquis would not see them.

She did not speak.

And after a moment he said,

"Have you never felt like that, Druscilla? Have you ever known what it is to want someone so much that the whole world is empty when they are not there? Have you never wished with your very soul to hear the sound of their voice, to watch their face and to know that if they are not happy then you cannot be happy either? Is that not love?"

She did not answer and he continued,

"Love, which makes another person so much more important than oneself and love which makes you ready to go down on your knees before them or to search the very ends of the earth so long as you can find them there."

Druscilla clenched her hands together.

How could she listen to him talking like this, how could she bear it?

Yes, yes, that was just what she felt was indeed love! When the happiness of someone else meant so much more than one's own feeble endeavours or desires.

He was like a child, she thought, a child who had clung to her in his delirium, who had cried out in the wildness of his fever, whom she had soothed, comforted and sent to sleep.

And because she loved him she must help him, whatever he asked of her.

She must make every sacrifice, whatever the cost, because only in that way could she prove to herself that the love she had for him was the noblest, the finest and the most beautiful experience that she had ever known.

She had shrunk from men and loathed them because of what they had done to her. But the Marquis was different.

He was a man, yet she loved him to the exclusion of all thoughts of self. She must not be jealous, she must want only his happiness and if he was happy what did anything else matter?

Twisting her hands together so that her fingers arched with the intensity of her grip she said quietly,

"I will help – you to find this – person if that will make you – happy. You must tell me what to – do and I will do it. The love such as you have for – her is obviously very – precious and I promise you – I will not stand in – your way."

"You will really help me?" the Marquis asked.

Druscilla nodded her head and, forcing back the tears from her eyes, turned round again.

"Yes, I will help – you," she said bravely, her chin held high, "but what can – I do?"

"You must find the woman who nursed me when I was so ill," the Marquis said, "for that is whom I love."

For a moment Druscilla could only stare at him holding her breath.

Then, because the immensity of what he had said overwhelmed her and because she felt a sudden glorious yet almost frightening elation creep over her, she turned once again to the window.

"But – s-she has – gone away," she murmured incoherently.

"If she has," the Marquis answered, "then I must find her. For I know now, Druscilla, that I shall never be happy unless she is with me and unless I can share my life with her."

"What – do you know – about – her?" Druscilla asked. "You were – not – conscious."

"I was conscious enough to know that only she could soothe me, that only she could lead me back to health. I was conscious enough to know that she was soft, warm and feminine and that she gave me everything a man wants from a woman. I know that she combined in herself all the tenderness and gentleness that a woman should have for a man and without which he is half an animal, brutal and cruel. For it is the woman he loves and who loves him, who brings to them both the beauty of life."

The Marquis stopped speaking and then he said gently,

"Will you not bring her to me, Druscilla?"

Druscilla was trembling with a strange sensation of insecurity and fear.

Yet she thought that the song of the birds outside was somehow intensified and the sunshine was almost too glorious to be borne.

"Come here, Druscilla," the Marquis commanded.

She could not move, feeling it impossible to turn and go to him as he had requested, the blood flowing into her face in a warm tide, a sudden quiver within herself as something awoke, something spiritual and too lovely even to be understood.

"Come here, Druscilla," the Marquis repeated masterfully, "or must I come and fetch you?"

She had a sudden fear that he might over-exert himself.

She turned hastily from the window and moved across the room, reaching his side before she realised that he was no longer sitting in the chair but standing waiting for her.

It seemed to her that the beating of her heart must suffocate her.

Then she looked up at him, her eyes very wide and dark, and was transfixed by the expression on his face.

"How did you – know?" she asked almost involuntarily.

"How do I know that this woman I speak about loves me?" the Marquis asked. "I know she does, Druscilla. I heard her say, as I awoke from the darkness, '*oh, my darling, if only I could give you some of my strength*'. Is that not love, when one will give one's very life to another person? Answer me, Druscilla, is it or is it not love?"

Druscilla's eyes dropped before his and she could only tremble.

After a moment he went on,

"You know that I cannot touch you until you ask me to do so. But there is something I want to ask you first, Druscilla, something that I have never asked you until now. Will you do me the very great honour of becoming my wife?"

She knew not only by his words but by the deep passion in his voice what he meant and for a moment because she could not breathe it was impossible for her to speak.

Then she raised her eyes to his and saw in his face all she had longed to see.

"Oh – Valdo!" she whispered and her voice broke on a sob.

In one swift movement she threw herself against him and hid her face against his shoulder.

"T-touch me – please – touch me," she begged, her words falling over themselves. "I did not – understand, I did not –

know what I – was doing – but I – l-love you, oh, Valdo – I love you so – agonisingly."

She felt the hard strength of the Marquis's arms.

Then, with her face still hidden against his shoulder, she felt his hand go to her hair, pulling out the hairpins and dropping them onto the carpet until wave upon wave of fiery silk fell over her shoulders and almost down to her waist.

Then very very gently the Marquis put his fingers under her chin and lifted her little face to his.

"Do you mean that, my darling?" he said, his voice hoarse and low. "Do you really mean you love me? I have been afraid, desperately afraid, that it was but a part of my delirium. I was looking for you and calling for you all the time I was unconscious. I thought I was in the woods and I had lost you, just as sometimes you hid from me when we were children together. And then when I felt your lips against my cheek and I heard your words, I knew what I have been seeking all my life."

"I loved you – too," Druscilla told him brokenly. "I never forgot – I always longed – for you, but when you – kissed me – I was afraid – "

"Let's forget it," the Marquis interrupted her. "Forget everything, Druscilla, except that we have found each other at last. I was so cork-brained I did not realise that I loved you until that night at Devonshire House when Walden insulted you and you asked me to save you. I knew then that we belonged to each other, but I was too hasty and I frightened you. I will never do that again."

"I will – never be – frightened again," Druscilla promised him. "Oh, Valdo – is this really – true?"

"It is true, my darling, my little love," he sighed holding her tighter and then very gently his mouth sought hers.

She knew that he meant his kiss to be one of tenderness, but when their lips touched a sudden flame awoke within them both and his mouth held her captive.

Suddenly he was kissing her wildly.

"Oh, Druscilla, stop me," he begged. "I shall frighten you again. I only want to love you as you wish to be loved."

Then her arms were round his neck and she was drawing him closer to her.

"Kiss me – " she murmured, "love me – oh, Valdo, this is – different, this is how – it was meant – to be! I love – you."

"And I adore you," he cried. "God, you are so beautiful, Druscilla, go on loving me, don't leave me, I want you so desperately."

He crushed her against him, his kisses now possessing her mouth with a passion that was not to be denied.

He kissed her lips, her eyes, her cheeks, her neck, her hair.

Then, as he felt her yielding body close against him, as he sensed the desire in her parted lips and as he saw that for the first time her eyes were heavy with passion, he said,

"I will make you happy, I swear to it! But, Druscilla, do you realise we are married? You are my wife, mine, and we are on our honeymoon."

He was still and tense waiting for her reply.

Shyly she hid her face against his shoulder, but he heard her whisper beneath her breath,

"Y-yes, Valdo – and I w-want – to be your – wife."

With a cry of triumph he swept her up in his arms, holding her high against his heart.

"Your shoulder! Oh, my darling, be careful of your shoulder!" she almost shouted.

But he did not hear her.

He was carrying her away through the open doorway into the bedroom and into the shadows of the great white bridal bed.

OTHER BOOKS IN THIS SERIES

The Barbara Cartland Eternal Collection is the unique opportunity to collect all five hundred of the timeless beautiful romantic novels written by the world's most celebrated and enduring romantic author.

Named the Eternal Collection because Barbara's inspiring stories of pure love, just the same as love itself, the books will be published on the internet at the rate of four titles per month until all five hundred are available.

The Eternal Collection, classic pure romance available worldwide for all time.

www.ingramcontent.com/pod-product-compliance
Lightning Source LLC
Chambersburg PA
CBHW022010170626
46808CB00001B/350